Discard /

MOON
Dancer

MARGARET I. ROSTKOWSKI

Browndeer Press

Harcourt Brace & Company

San Diego   New York   London

Requests for permission to make copies of any part of the work
should be mailed to: Permissions Department, Harcourt Brace &
Company, 6277 Sea Harbor Drive, Orlando, Florida 32887-6777.

Browndeer Press is a registered trademark of
Harcourt Brace & Company.

Library of Congress Cataloging-in-Publication Data
Rostkowski, Margaret I.
Moon dancer / by Margaret I. Rostkowski.—1st ed.
p.   cm.
Summary: Miranda, a nature loving, athletic fifteen-year-old,
goes on a backpacking trip to look for Indian paintings in the
canyons of southern Utah, where she feels a mystical
connection to the women who were there before her.
ISBN 0-15-276638-3   ISBN 0-15-200194-8 (pbk.)
[1. Backpacking—Fiction. 2. Rock climbing—Fiction. 3. Rock
paintings—Fiction. 4. Indians of North America—Fiction.
5. Utah—Fiction.]   I. Title.
PZ7.R7237Mo   1995
[Fic]—dc20   94-39553

The text was set in Garamond Light.
Designed by Lydia D'moch

First edition
A B C D E
A B C D E (pbk.)

Printed in Hong Kong

*To my mother, Charlotte Ellis,
and to my sister Carlisle Ellis*

Thanks to Rob Van Wagoner

"It is not often that someone comes along
who is a true friend and a good writer."
—E. B. WHITE, *Charlotte's Web*

MY FATHER HAS OFTEN SAID that someday he and my mother would die and that I should always be friends with my sister, Jenny, since finally we would only have each other. I used to think all the time about what he said, not only because it bothered me that anyone could speak so casually about death, but also because the words *we would only have each other* sounded so lonely. The thought of having only one other person shook my heart.

The summer I turned sixteen, I discovered that my father's words don't have to be true for me. Even if Jenny is a big part of my life when

we are old, and I hope she is, she doesn't have to be everything. If I remember all I learned that summer from three women who died long before I was born, I will never be lonely, even if I am alone.

It all happened in a canyon in southern Utah, in the company of Jenny; our twenty-one-year-old cousin, Emily; and Max Stanley, Emily's friend from the university. The minute he stepped out of his Jeep, Jenny whispered to me that Max wasn't much in the face but he sure did a lot for that particular pair of jeans. That tells you more about Jenny than it does about Max.

At first we all acted a little stiff with each other, smiling a lot as we unloaded gear from the cars and stretched out the cramps of the seven-hour drive from Salt Lake City. Jenny and I hadn't seen Emily since spring break, and even though we had been together a lot through the years, she was a university *woman* and she had this *guy* with her. We were high-school *girls*.

Around us lay sagebrush and red rock and over us hung a huge blue sky. Off to the side of the ranger station and parking lot, the cabin waited under its juniper and cottonwood shade.

Katie's cabin. Katie Weston, the reason we were here: she'd lived here all alone a hundred years ago, exploring the canyon, talking to rocks and ghosts, living close to the edge. From the moment I first heard her name, I couldn't forget her. Now Emily was writing a paper about Katie Weston, so we had come to live for four days in her canyon, her sky and rock, her world.

You never know what's waiting for you around the next hour. I've learned that. There I was, unloading the car and worrying about the buckle on my backpack, not knowing that because of the guy in the jeans, the three long-dead women, and the red rock canyon, I would learn ways of living, and celebrating, in a world that I had not even imagined existed.

CHAPTER
1

I HAD THOUGHT we would jump out of the car and start hiking, but I was wrong. There's a lot of standing around and messing with equipment before you start a backpacking trip. At least that's how Emily was running this one. She leaned on the car to talk to Max for a while, then she had to check in at the ranger station and get a map of the gulch, then she had to show us the map with the route we would take from where we were at Bear Mountain Ranger Station to where we'd come out four days from now at Kane Junction. Finally she opened various bags and bottles and we all had a snack. It didn't look as if we were getting started anytime soon.

I wanted to get gone. I hate any leaving, that feeling of being suspended, my feet halfway out the door. I wanted to be down that trail a mile. But I wasn't in charge. This was definitely Emily's trip, so I tried to relax and look friendly.

Once we'd chatted and snacked and read the map, Emily wanted to check our packs. "Nothing worse than an overweight pack on a trip like this," she said.

"Nothing?" Jenny slanted her eyes at Max and grinned. "Well, what about . . ."

"Miranda, you first."

I didn't have anything to worry about. I'd been reading backpacker's guides since Christmas, when Mom first mentioned this trip, and I knew what I was doing. I'd even sawed off the end of my toothbrush to save weight. I did have a book, but I wouldn't give that up, even if Emily yelled at me. She didn't, just tucked it under my extra bungee cord and smiled at me. "You haven't changed, little Mira," she said.

I felt myself grow hot and I glanced at Max, but he didn't seem to have heard. I hoped I wouldn't have to be *little Mira* this whole trip.

"OK, Jenny. You're next."

"Sure, whatever." She waved to the pack leaning against the car.

"You unpack it," Emily said.

Jenny smiled at her, that half smile she's been practicing all seventeen years of her life, and then got up and knelt by the pack. "What do you want to see?"

Emily opened the pack and peered inside. "Take it all out," she said.

Jenny began pulling things out, dropping them on the ground: shirts and shorts and plastic bottles, three single socks, packets of raisins, a collapsible aluminum cup, tapes and a Walkman, more T-shirts, two pairs of sandals, a whole plastic bag full of bottles and tubes of who-knows-what.

"Jenny, this is a mess. It looks like you just threw everything in here."

Jenny pulled out a pair of panties, held them for just a little too long on the very tip of her finger, then flipped them onto the pile. "Yeah, I did sort of throw it all in." She cleared her throat and glanced up at Max, who was watching. "I had *other* stuff to do, you know."

She didn't look at me. I knew that the "stuff" had been breaking up with her latest boyfriend until three this morning and that she had thrown everything in the backseat of the car and packed, sort of, on the drive down. I drove. Even without

driver's training or a license, I drive better than Jenny does on a good day. Jenny's only advantage over me is that she can talk her way out of a ticket.

Jenny looked at Max and then Emily, that smile there again.

"Well, repack," said Emily. "You'll hold us up every morning trying to find your stuff. Besides, you don't want that extra weight." She walked away.

"Hey, wait, Emily! What do I take?" Jenny poked at the pile. "It's not as if I've done this before."

"Look," said Max, squatting down in front of her. "You're going to be walking for four days. Take only what you absolutely need for comfort and safety. Everything else should stay. You have to carry it all in and out. You can't leave *anything* down there. This isn't Mount Everest."

"Well, obviously. What's that supposed to mean?"

"People dump stuff up there. It's a real sewer these days."

"Is he kidding?" she said to me.

I didn't answer. I didn't know about Mount Everest *or* this guy.

He stood up. "You OK now?"

She squinted up at him and smiled, one of her perky, aren't-I-adorable numbers. "I guess so. Thanks."

He nodded and turned away, cool enough to stop and tuck in his shirt, even though he must have known we would both be watching him. Jenny did look at his walk and then laughed. "Hey, little Mira, stop panting and help me."

I tossed a packet of raisins at her. "Clean up your own mess. And don't call me little Mira."

While Jenny heaved and sighed over her pack, I walked over to take a look at Katie's cabin. Not much to see: one room, a fireplace, a window on each side of the door, a wood floor, a corral out back, and three cottonwood trees hanging over the roof. I stood with my hand on the wall and put myself in that room for years of baking summers and freezing winters, of sleepless nights with the ferocious canyon wind that I know so well from home, of days filled with the clouds of grasshoppers that billowed around our feet. What made Katie want to live here?

"Emily," I called, and she came over to where I stood. "What happened to Katie?"

"She died when she was only forty-one. She fell off a horse and broke her hip, then got pneumonia and died up in Blanding."

"How'd you find this out?"

"Her niece still lives up there, so I interviewed her for the oral history part of my research. She's a sweet old lady named Gladys Weston. Even though she's over ninety, she still remembers her aunt and how she wanted so badly to go back to her cabin, back here, even when she was dying." Emily touched one wall of the cabin carefully. "So sad. She wanted to come back to *this!* If I were Katie, I'd have been happy to be in civilization for once. Clean sheets and water." She wiped her hands and turned back to me. "Gladys said she kept talking about the moon and the little village. She was probably delirious." Emily shrugged. "Anyone who sees ghosts . . ."

"Ghosts of who?"

"The ancient people who built the stuff we'll be seeing."

"I can see why she didn't want to leave. This place is . . . I don't know. Kind of cool?"

Emily groaned. "Don't tell me you're going to be another one."

"One what?"

"People who come down here and then never want to leave. I have a professor like that. There's another one." She nodded at Max, who was coiling ropes and looping them around the frame of his pack, carefully tucking and patting, obviously very sure of what he was doing. She put her arm around my shoulder. "Well, honey, you can have it, along with the nine billion grasshoppers and ten thousand miles of dust. I want to do my research and go home."

Max looked up at her. "Hey, Emily, clean sheets aren't the only thing in life, are they?"

"Speak for yourself," she tossed back to him.

I ran my hand over the rough wood one last time and thought about Katie, dying in a strange place, wanting to be here. I don't think I had ever known anyone who had loved a *place* that much. I turned away and saw that Max was watching me, even while he still coiled and tucked his stuff. He looked like a pro.

"So have you done this a lot before?" I asked.

"Not in the desert. I've done a lot of rock climbing around Salt Lake and up in the Tetons. But a rock's a rock, I guess." He didn't stop working while he talked, and he didn't even look up at me. He was very cool.

Jenny finally stood up and called to Emily

that she was ready. Once they'd gone over her pack again and I'd helped her tie it up, all the little laces and grommets just so, we were ready to get it on her. I told her to stand and put the pack on, so I could show her how tight all the straps should be. Just as I had it hoisted shoulder-high, with Jenny bent a little so I could reach her shoulder, the pack slipped, shifted, and toppled over to one side. Before I could catch it, it fell into the sand.

"Oh, hell," said Jenny, and plopped into the dirt beside her pack.

Max looked off at the distant mountains and Emily stood watching us.

The Galbraith sisters. Klutzes of the world. I hauled the pack up again, waited while Jenny dusted herself off, and we finally got her loaded.

"You belong at home, mall surfing," I muttered while I helped her buckle her waist strap. "We're going to hold them up the whole way."

"No, we'll be good for them," whispered Jenny. "They're both way too serious."

I took a breath and turned around. "OK," I said.

"Sorry," caroled Jenny. "Like I said, I'm kind of new at this."

At last we were ready.

Except for one thing.

Emily pulled her camera out of the bag. "Ready for a picture?" she asked, clapping her hands like an overeager soccer coach. "A group shot before we head out, OK?"

She grouped us in front of the brown ranger station sign, told us each where to stand, made us take off our hats so our faces wouldn't be in shadow (which meant Jenny had to fuss with her hair a bit). Then she made me point out our route on the big map behind us. Once her energy had snapped us into shape, she hovered over her tripod, making the tiny adjustments photography seems to require, all the movements I'd watched my own mother make for years. Then Emily stepped back, said she'd set the timer for fifteen seconds, told us to smile, and started toward us. At the last second, just as she was about to step in next to Max, Jenny made her move, right up next to Max, and leaned into him, one hand draped casually on his shoulder. Emily barely had time to slide in next to me.

I didn't have time to check the expression on my face before the shutter clicked.

Emily, a women's studies major at the University of Utah, was doing her senior project on women homesteaders of the West. My mother, who photographed and researched women's lives, had just discovered Katie Weston's journal in a museum in Colorado. During last year's Christmas dinner at Dad's house, Mom had leaned over her glass of wine and told us that people thought Katie was crazy during her life. "She told a few people in town about the Indian drawings she'd found down this canyon and no one believed her—they said she'd gone round the bend. So before she died, she sent her journal to a Colorado expert on ancient people. Otherwise, it all would have been lost. Emily, you should do your paper on her. I'll never get around to Katie's story. I have projects lined up until the twenty-first century." Mom sighed.

"Only that long? Why, Joan, you're slipping," Dad said, and Jenny snorted. Our parents were friendly (for divorced people) but they loved to dig at each other when they could.

Mom ignored Dad. "Go ahead, Emily. Go to

Katie's Gulch. It's a magical place, I hear, great for climbing and taking pictures and exploring. I wish I could go with you." Mom twisted her watchband. "I know!" She put on her smile, the one much like Jenny's, the one I'd try hard never to learn. "Jenny could go with you."

Jenny almost knocked over her wineglass. "No way! Miranda can go."

"Take them both," said Dad. "Give me some peace." He winked at me and nudged Jenny next to him at the table. "Sounds great."

I am always ready to take off for anywhere and a backpacking trip was something new. As I sat in Dad's cozy house, warm and well-fed, it seemed an adventure, if a scary one. Besides, I have always loved Indian stuff.

Jenny needed convincing. Four days of heat and dust and walking was not anywhere on her list of good ideas, and Emily was at the top of her list of awful people. Emily hovered on the edge of our lives, not around often but a constant possibility. A constant threat, Jenny would say. Emily was the perfect student, the best daughter, the most responsible being on the planet, according to her parents. But she could never beat Jenny for looks or sheer pizzazz. I'd watched her

watch Jenny and I knew that neither of them liked the other much.

So to bring these two together, Dad had to agree to the senior trip to Mazatlán Jenny had been begging for. And Mom told Emily she'd get her a copy of Katie's journal from the historical society. Maybe she'd told Emily, "No Jenny, no journal."

"Makes you wonder, doesn't it?" said Jenny when Emily showed us the photocopied sheets of the journal. "I wonder why Mother dear cares so much about this Katie person."

Emily frowned. "Don't be so negative, Jenny. Your mom's just being nice."

"Look, Emily, your aunt Joan doesn't *do* nice. She looks out for herself. Trust me, I know my mother better than you do."

Emily looked disgusted. "Look, your mother told me that she had admired Katie ever since she first heard about her on one of her trips down there. She just wants Katie's life and work to be recorded." Emily patted the journal. "It's nothing sinister, OK?"

It didn't matter to me why Mom had bothered with Emily's project or that Dad had maneuvered to have a week of no phone calls, a

clean kitchen, and the car for himself. This trip gave me something to do at the start of summer, a time when I always feel loose and empty, sleep and eat too much, and read so many mysteries that I can't remember anything about them the next day.

And there was Katie. A woman my mother admired. Ever since I was little, I have always loved to read and think about people like Amelia Earhart, Sacagawea, Queen Elizabeth I. But it seemed strange to me that my mother had a hero, especially a woman like Katie Weston, who hid away in the wilderness and didn't do anything particularly spectacular except listen to bird talk and keep a journal. And it also seemed strange that my mother cared that Jenny and I knew about her.

As we left Katie's cabin that June day, I led the way. I wanted to be out front, to set the pace, to get this show on the road. For the first fifteen minutes, I crossed a flat mesa covered with scrubby-looking pine trees. Then the trail got steeper and dropped into a slit in the earth that I hadn't seen from the cabin. As the earth rose up on either side of me, I had to walk around

boulders that jutted out into the trail. Now it looked like a canyon.

Behind me, no one talked. We walked in single file, focused on avoiding the smooth rocks that bulged out of the dust, on sweeping aside the branches of the shoulder-high willows that lined the trail.

It was hot. Every time I passed under the slim shade of a juniper, I felt a breath of cool, and then the slam of the heat made me blink. Sweat filmed my upper lip, trickled down my forehead, and edged my scalp. After three o'clock and still this hot! I shaded my eyes and found the sun high above the canyon wall. The red rock baked the air around us.

The worst was the sting of sweat in my eyes. I kept stopping to wipe my face, until I heard Max behind me quietly say my name.

"Here." He handed me a bandanna. "Tie it around your forehead. Really helps." He wore a green one twisted beneath his hairline.

"You carry extras?"

"Yeah." He pulled three more out of his pocket. "You never know when you'll need one. Or three." He had a lopsided smile. And a few freckles across his nose. Jenny was wrong. He was *a lot* to look at in the face.

Just then Emily called. "Max! Wait up." We both turned, just in time to hear the shutter click. Emily lowered her camera and waved as she clumped past us. "Thanks," she said, all cheer.

"Warn me next time, OK?" Max shouted to her. "So we can stick our tongues out," he said to me.

I was beginning to be awfully glad he'd come on this trip.

He followed Emily while I waited for Jenny, who was muttering about her "aching legs." The rest of us were quiet and after a while Jenny quit her complaining.

When I run a distance race, I always wait for the rhythm and know once I find it that everything will go right. Now I found the rhythm of this kind of walking: how the pack rode my back and hips, how secure my running shoes felt on the slick rock, how my arms and legs swung together as I walked. Once I felt it, I could look around me. The sides of the canyon began at my feet and folded up on both sides, smooth, like pillows of red rock. I looked up to see how high the sky was, to see how deep inside the earth we had dropped since Katie's cabin. What did the map say? Three hundred feet at the deepest.

It took us two hours to go three miles, so it was almost five o'clock when we saw the green mist of trees in a slant of sun shafting down between the walls. The trail flattened out, and soon we crossed a stretch of sand and rock and found a pool of water. Not a rushing brook, but water. Wet and cool.

"We camp here," said Emily.

"Thank you, God," said Jenny.

When I dropped my pack, my body felt like air.

CHAPTER
2

JENNY SLID HER PACK down beside mine and slumped down on it, groaning. She grabbed her canteen, took a long drink, wiped her face, took another drink, then lay down, sprawled out across both bags. "I'm going to sleep for an hour. Don't bother me, anybody."

"Sorry, Jenny. Work to do first," said Emily.

Jenny sat up. "Work? What work?"

Emily was pointing. "Sleep there, don't you think, Max?"

He nodded.

"And we'll cook over here." She set her bag down on a clear space. "Miranda, you want to find some flat rocks for the pots?"

Suddenly three of us were busy, unzipping packs and laying out sleeping bags, airing socks and shoes, boiling water for tea, setting up camp, as if we would be there a week. Three little settlements: Emily's matching pine green back-pack and camera bag (obviously new and expensive), Max's red pack with only his hiking boots and ropes beside it, and the Galbraith encampment. I'd dropped my stuff into a mess, so I hurried to straighten it, to match Emily and Max's tidiness, but Jenny's blue-and-yellow sleeping bag lay sprawled by her gaping pack with bandanna, shoes and socks, and the peel from the orange she was eating strewn over everything. Jenny herself sat slumped on her bag until Emily told her to get busy, that it would get dark soon, and she wouldn't be able to find anything. Also she wouldn't get any dinner if she didn't help.

"Oh, dinner. Big wow. Petrified chicken and mummified peas." She shook out her sleeping bag, her silver bracelets tinkling and glistening. "I can hardly wait." Another shake of bracelets, this time under her hair. "Brown goo blended with stale water to make delicious chewy brownies." She stepped over to her pack and pulled

out the bag of tapes, stuck one in her Walkman, and then put her hands on her hips and looked around. "So where do you go to the bathroom around here?"

Emily put her arm around Jenny's shoulder and said, "Let's talk. There are a lot of environmental concerns with this. You should be at least three yards from any water source and you have to bury everything. *Everything!*" As I walked away from camp, I heard Jenny groan.

I followed the streambed, found some flat rocks for Emily's fire, found a rock with unusual stripes, and put it in my pocket. When I got back to camp, Max told me I'd be sorry if I loaded up my pockets with rocks.

"Anyway, this is a national monument. You're not supposed to take anything out of the canyon."

"Not even rocks?" I asked, realizing that he must have been watching me again.

He shook his head.

"Like they're going to miss one?" I smiled up at him, hoping to make it a joke, and he flicked a smile at me. I put the rock back.

Not a bad evening. Jenny complained about the hard ground, sighed, and looked at her

watch and talked about what she'd be doing if she were home. We all ignored her, and when Max pointed to the top of the cliffs where the last sun was turning the rock pink, I wondered why Jenny couldn't just shut up and look around her. But she never had been big on what she called the tourist view of the world.

Dinner turned out to be close to what Jenny had predicted. Not terrible, but definitely not the best I'd tasted. Max ate a lot and said as he scraped the pot, "You don't backpack for the food. If you want great food, you go on river trips. Those people eat well."

"What runs have you done?" asked Emily.

"Only one, down the Green River." Max turned down the propane stove. "I didn't like it. A lot of drinking and such."

"And such?" said Jenny. "What does that mean?"

"Well, people got naked and, well . . . just too much noise and partying for me. I can do that at home. I come out here to be quiet and think."

"Sounds like I came on the wrong trip," muttered Jenny, but I wondered how much partying Max did. And who he did it with.

"So, Jenny, what have you been doing these days?" asked Emily.

Besides bitching, I thought.

"Working, going to school, bugging Dad, putting up with my obnoxious sister."

"Where do you work?"

"Soup-n-Greens. In Newgate Mall."

"Cute name," said Emily.

"Oh, it's a cute place. I'm on the salad bar. If I'm really good, I'll get to wait tables, but I doubt I'll last that long. I hate it."

"Why?"

"It's work. And I don't get tips. Except"—and she sat up, beginning to sparkle as only Jenny can sparkle—"there's this one old man who always comes in at five o'clock, right when I get there, and he always slips a dollar bill in my pocket. He's so darling. And it's fun to bet how many times certain people will come back and refill their plates." And she was off. All about what they do with the food no one eats (Throw it away. Max groaned.); about the regular customers, mostly old people who love her; about the kids who stuff crackers in their pockets and the people who try to come back through the line

even though they'd only paid for one time around.

In the light from the stove, with her graceful swoops of one bracelet-covered arm and the blue bandanna tied low over her forehead, Jenny looked like a blond gypsy. She burbled and laughed and chirped, totally conscious of every look Max gave her, of his long legs stretched out across from us, of how the light glistened on his dark hair.

She finished off by telling about a dark, handsome man who came in every Monday night, filled a plate with cherry tomatoes, and then ate them slowly while staring straight at her where she stood behind the sneeze guard. When she finished, she glittered at Emily, then sighed. "That's my life."

Both Emily and Max looked a little dazed for a minute, then Emily turned to me and said, "What about you, little—"

"I just study and try to stay out of Jenny's way."

"Still running?"

I nodded.

"What do you run?" asked Max.

"Cross country in the fall. The mile and mile relay during track season."

"Miranda's a jock," said Jenny.

"I ran cross country in high school," said Max.

"Two jocks," said Jenny. "Am I the only sensible person here? What do you do for fun these days, Emily? Lift weights, I suppose?"

"No, I gave that up for wrestling." They smiled at each other, tight little smiles.

"Well," said Emily after an awkward pause, "you guys want to hear a little more about Katie? Why we're here and how you can help me with my project?" She pulled out her notebook and the journal. "We only have four days, so we're all going to have to keep our eyes open. If you don't mind."

"What are we looking for?" asked Max.

"OK, let me tell you. Katie Weston came here with her husband, Michael, and they homesteaded up there, in that cabin. They had a lot of problems, moved back to town, worked in a store, stuff I'm not interested in. Then Michael died."

"How'd he die?" I asked.

She shrugged. "Don't know. Anyway, Katie

came back here by herself and lived here the rest of her life. And get this—she was only eighteen when she came back here. Three years younger than I am."

"My age," said Max.

"So how old was she when she got married?" asked Jenny.

"Probably about seventeen," said Emily.

"Bummer. I hope he was cute, at least."

Emily obviously ignored most of what Jenny said. "That's what makes my project so exciting. Not only a woman homesteading alone but a really *young* woman."

"But she lived way back up there. Why are we down here?" I asked.

"She spent a lot of time down here exploring, and she was the first to record the rock art in this gulch. See, back then people were just finding out about all the Anasazi stuff. I mean the Hisatsinom stuff."

"What's the difference?"

"Same thing. *Anasazi* is a Navajo word. Means 'ancient enemy.' The Hopis call them *Hisatsinom,* 'those who came before.' "

"I like that better," I said.

"It's more accurate. The Hopis descended from these people."

"Finish about Katie," said Jenny. "So she found this stuff. So why the big deal?"

"Because there's some wonderful rock art down this very gulch. You'll love it. Neat animal panels and some great people: a woman giving birth—"

"Giving birth? They put that on a wall?"

"Yes. And it's not a normal birth, either. Wait till you see it."

"I can wait, believe me." Jenny yawned.

"The great thing, what makes this really exciting, is these." Emily held out the journal and motioned us to come around her so we could see. The page had no writing, just sketches: animals, circles, spirals, dotted lines, figures that looked like people, even though some of them had no heads. Emily turned the page: more figures, shapes, lines. Then hands, more hands, a page of hands and feet. She turned another page and this time I saw circles, what looked like drawings of the moon.

"Those are amazing," said Max. "Will we see those?"

Emily looked up at us. "If we can find them. Katie drew all this, so we *think* it shows what she saw down here. But since some of the drawings, like these moons, have never been

found, we don't know if they're in this canyon or if she just imagined them. My project is to match up her drawings with what is actually here."

"Why hasn't anyone else ever done it?"

"Oh, people have. Some of these, the birth panel for example, are very well known. But the rest of this canyon is not that well explored. See, every canyon and gulch for miles around here is loaded with these drawings and ruins. Archaeologists have just started working on them. Katie is just one piece of the puzzle."

We stared for a minute at the lantern glow.

"Her niece said her family always thought Katie was a bit strange, wanting to live out here all alone like she did." Emily snorted. "Gladys said there were any number of young men who would have taken to Katie if she'd shown any interest at all. But she didn't. So, of course, they thought she was crazy. You know, all a woman needs is a good man."

"OK, Em, just relax." Max picked up the journal. "Does she sound crazy in here?"

"The journal is actually kind of boring—just facts, dates, stuff about the homestead, her cattle and horses and money, so it's hard to tell. She was always worrying about money."

"Hey, everybody worries about money," said Max. He riffled the pages.

"She had trouble keeping her fences repaired, so her cattle kept wandering away. She discovered all this when she followed some down here. Then she started copying what she found and filled the back of the journal with these drawings."

"I wish you knew more about what she was like or what she looked like," I said. "If we could just get into her mind and find out what she was thinking when she was down here."

"You're sure you want to get in her mind?" asked Max. "You might not get out again."

"I'm not so much concerned with what was in her mind as where she found these things. That's what I need for my paper." Emily sighed.

"She sounds so . . . I don't know." I imagined Katie Weston sitting here at the fire, ready to lead us into her gulch, ready to share her discoveries. "What a cool story." I sighed.

"Well, not everybody agrees, apparently," said Max, and pointed at Jenny. She was asleep, head down on her arms, bandanna pulled over her eyes.

Emily humphed a little. I shook my sister awake and put up with her grumpiness while I

led her to her sleeping bag. I was glad Emily had made us lay out our stuff before it got dark because once Max turned down the lantern, the night got black. I did my stuff out in the bushes, stripped down to panties and T-shirt, glad of the dark because I wasn't quite sure where Max was, then got in my sleeping bag and looked up.

Blackness swooped up around me into sky and stars. More stars than I had ever seen before.

Once when I was very little, Dad and I took a night drive together and I asked him why there were so many more stars out in the country than at home, and he said there were more chickens out there to lay the eggs in the sky. I believed him.

As I lay there with the bag pulled to my chin more for comfort than for warmth, I thought of those chickens and felt a moment of longing for that warm, dark car and my dad beside me. For just a moment, I felt dizzy and sick to my stomach as if the earth had tipped under me and I had nothing to grab hold of.

I closed my eyes. I wondered if Katie had ever felt the earth and sky so big around her she got dizzy.

I always like to find one exact word to de-

scribe people, to sum up all of their parts. What about Katie? *Lonely?* I wasn't sure. *Sad?* I didn't think so. *Independent?* Accurate, but not enough. For now, *mysterious* covered Katie.

Emily wasn't hard to find a word for. *Capable* fit her exactly. I'd trust her with my life, even if I didn't want to share very much of it with her.

Jenny is the one person I haven't been able to find one word for, probably because I know too much about her. So I have given up trying.

Max?

Just for a moment I let myself picture him, hands behind his head, watching the stars, just as I was. I saw him only in shadow, not allowing myself to know if he was still wearing the plaid shirt or if it lay under his head and he was . . .

I didn't sleep for a while. And I wasn't thinking about words.

CHAPTER
3

I woke up suddenly, unsure for the first second before I opened my eyes why the air felt so different from the air in my room at home. Then I saw sky and blue right above me, close enough to touch. For that moment I wanted to slide farther down in the bag, pull the drawstring around my face, and hide.

I looked all around me and when I saw the rose stone, again I felt that same earth-tipping dizziness. Then it passed and I breathed in and in. I sat up and stretched.

I'd slept out at home a lot, but waking up had never been like this. What would it be like

to see this every morning of my life, to wake up to such a ceiling? The air moved up high, where it curved around the rock before it swooped down into my mouth and lungs. The sun hadn't reached me yet, but blazed on the rocks above me, mixing heat and light and . . . something else. Smell, sound, taste . . . something that made me shake. Something so strange but so welcome.

I curled my arms around my knees and took a moment to let it all come into me. I wondered if Katie had ever stayed down here, away from the constant work and worry she must have had every day. I know what worry can do to you, how it can tighten your chest so you can't breathe; only my worries aren't about lost cows and money but about passing tests and running races and just . . . getting through days.

I stretched again. Nothing to worry about here. For the first time I felt *really* glad I had come. Glad in that way that makes my bones feel lighter, that makes me want to get up and *do* things.

I sat up and pushed my bag down around my ankles and straightened my T-shirt before I stood up. Toilet paper, soap, towel, clothes: I

gathered them all, stuck my feet in my running shoes, and headed up the trail toward the stand of willows. "Going to the bathroom" wasn't exactly accurate for what I had to do next. I already knew that this part of camping I didn't particularly like. But camping did make other things simple: unless you were *really* obsessed about your looks, like one person I knew intimately, all that mattered in the outdoors was staying a little bit clean.

Birds loud above me; willows rustling as I brushed past; faint smell of damp from the sand. A miniature frog sprang up from between my feet as I stooped to wash.

I understood more and more why Katie loved it so. Maybe *I* could live here.

No sign of anyone else. I didn't want to run the risk of seeing anyone, of having to talk, so after I'd washed and dressed, I left my stuff by the side of the pool, tied my shoes, and walked back up the bank, where I turned down the trail away from our camp. I walked faster, then began to jog, lightly, easily. The trail lay smooth and even. OK, if I didn't go too fast.

I was just beginning to feel my muscles loosen, to feel the rhythm, when I tripped, stum-

bled, almost fell, and had to slow down. And then I saw him: clinging on the slope of the cliff twenty feet off to my right, hands and arms tucked in front of him, legs spread wide, feet wedged in toeholds. I stopped still, put a hand over my mouth to quiet my breath. I felt that jolt you get when you realize that you've been thinking about something and trying to *avoid* thinking about it at the same time.

I'd spent a lot of time during the past few months *not* looking at men's bodies—concentrating only on the rules of whatever game we were playing in coed gym, flipping rapidly through the ads in Dad's *Esquire,* looking only at my English teacher's eyes. But the more I didn't look, the more I seemed to think. I knew from sex-ed classes two years ago in eighth grade, and from my dad's careful discussions, that this was all perfectly normal, all a stage I should be in at age almost-sixteen. Nice to know I was normal when I felt anything *but.*

Now here, right in front of me, free for the looking, was a man's body and I could look all I wanted, *if* I wanted. And I did, so I looked and I saw his long back stretching beneath the blue shirt and the long, muscled legs and the tight

behind. Then I started to notice what he was doing with all that body. He looked sure and very concentrated, his whole body balanced there under his fingertips.

He moved slowly but smoothly, hands and feet finding their way across the rock as if they knew exactly where to go. He didn't hesitate once. He made something terrifying beyond imagination look as natural as a spider crawling across the face of the rock. And he looked so beautiful, doing this dangerous thing, with arms strong enough to hold him up forever and fingers quick and light across the rock face.

I stood and watched, afraid every second that he would turn around and see me but knowing he couldn't turn around and that even if he did, it was OK for me to watch him. I wasn't doing anything wrong.

I couldn't leave as long as he still hung there. The air cooled my skin and I shivered a little, hugging myself and jogging in place as I watched him move along the rock. I love watching someone doing a hard thing with such confidence and skill that the task looks easy: Mr. Palmer pulling a pot in ceramics class, my dad playing Chopin's "Revolutionary Etude," a friend doing

barrel turns on her cow pony. It's weird, but that kind of thing comes into me in a way I can't explain. The pull between ease and effort builds to a tension that gets close to pain. I guess I feel it in that moment in a race when I think I can't take another step and just then I feel the burst of energy that tells me I'm going to finish strong.

Watching Max gave me that feeling.

He pulled himself in and over a rock, where he crouched a minute before he turned and saw me and waved. I waved back. I almost yelled out the words I was thinking: That was beautiful, Max! Fortunately, I wasn't that far gone and so caught myself and instead just waved again and turned back toward camp.

Emily was up, bending over the stove, pot in one hand, rolled-up bandanna in the other, boiling water, setting out oatmeal and cocoa packets. She looked all trim: hair combed, shoe-laces tied and socks turned down twice, T-shirt tucked into her shorts, tiny silver earrings her only jewelry. More confidence and ease. Suddenly my face felt faintly dirty.

"Hey," I said.

She turned. "Hey, yourself. You're up early. You sleep OK?"

"I did. Did you?"

She groaned. "Are you kidding? That ground is *hard*."

"But don't you do this a lot?"

"Used to. When I was a kid. Girl Scouts, re-member?"

"Oh, right. Scouts."

"Juice?" She held up a baggy of powder.

"OK. Let me mix it."

"Yeah, Scouts with your mom. Remember, she took us all camping that one summer when she was back in town?"

"I didn't go. I was too little." I stirred the powder into my drink.

"Well, that was the start for me. Now I only do camping when I have to. Even so, Aunt Joan taught me so much about so many things. I ad-mire her. I hope to be like her."

"I'd rather be like Jack the Ripper." From behind me, Jenny reached out and took the cup of juice from me, gulped a mouthful, and spit it out.

"Sand." She spit again, then scrubbed her tongue with the hem of her T-shirt. "In my mouth. Yuck."

"Good morning, Jenny," said Emily.

Jenny glared at her. "When you wake up with sand in your mouth, it is *not* a good morning. Trust me."

She headed up the trail, clutching her clothes and towel to her chest. "Don't forget the t.p.!" I yelled after her. She stopped, wheeled, stalked back to our bags, found the t.p., glared at us again, and stalked away into the bushes.

She didn't turn when I yelled, "Thanks for the thanks." Next time she could use leaves.

"She's so fun," said Emily, making a face. "Breakfast is ready. Now, where's Max?"

I didn't want to say that I knew where he was, so I didn't answer, just went to gather up the things I'd left by the pool. And, as if I'd planned it, Max came down that very streambed and we walked back to camp together. We didn't talk about big stuff, just about the morning and the birds and all that, but the look Jenny gave me from the rock where she'd folded herself over a cup of cocoa told me she thought we'd been off making it in the weeds.

Then Emily didn't help Jenny's mood by going on about what great breakfasts Aunt Joan made on their camping trip: the fresh fruit, the pancakes with powdered sugar and syrup.

"Did she bring the linen napkins?" Jenny finally asked, making Emily frown and shake her head. "Well, darn! We *always* use linen napkins at home."

That shut Emily up. Smart as she was, she was a little dense on the subject of our mother.

We got through breakfast by avoiding Jenny's mood, which was as obvious as a brown spot on an apple, and by making jokes about the gooey oatmeal and the warm juice. Somehow, though, it tasted better than last night's dinner.

When Emily got out the map to plan our day, Max said that he'd seen what looked like a building on the cliff across the gulch and he wanted to do a little more exploring. "Might be something there."

"Is it much of a climb?" asked Emily.

"No, just up a slope of loose rock. We could all do it."

"Not all of us," said Jenny. "I'm not climbing any loose rock."

"So you can help Max with cleanup," said Emily cheerfully, and before Jenny could do more than groan, Emily and I had gathered shoes, canteens, and Emily's camera and taken off down the trail. I'd climbed enough at home

to do this, and the slope Max had pointed out to us wasn't bad at all. Emily did seem to have more trouble than I'd expected; she was even willing to take my hand in two tight places. Together we made it and had barely caught our breath when Max arrived, not even breaking a sweat.

"Fast cleanup," said Emily. "Did Jenny help?"

"Sure. Why wouldn't she?"

Emily shrugged, but Max had already turned away. "Now take a look at this baby."

He pointed to a little building that clung to the side of the cliff, inches away from the edge. It only had three walls of poorly made brick with a T-shaped doorway so low Max had to bend double to get in. Emily immediately went inside and sat down. She seemed out of breath.

"Did they live way up here?" I asked, feeling suddenly chilled in the shadow and by the thought of people living on a cliff, perched so dangerously over space.

"No, this was for storage."

"Two years' supply?"

When our Mormon neighbors showed us their basement shelves lined with a two years' supply of pinto beans, rice, wheat, and so forth,

Dad would say that all we had in our basement was a week's supply of dill pickles, plum jam, and cat food. But now I wished I hadn't opened my mouth. It was an old joke among our friends and family, but I didn't know about Max. He was probably a Mormon elder, fresh back from a mission. If so, I'd just insulted him.

But he laughed and Emily said, "No, not that kind of supply. They kept stashes all over the gulches, to supply runners or in case of attack. Look." She bent down and sifted her fingers through the dusty floor: tiny corncobs, seeds, bits of pottery, bits of bone.

"Oh, cool." I knelt beside her. "They were really here. Real people."

"Real little people. Look at how small those corncobs are." Max held one up.

"And the pottery. Look at the designs." Emily pointed to a gray shard with a corrugated surface.

"Hey, Em, look," said Max. He flicked on his flashlight and swept the light up the rock behind us. A line of handprints, one above the other, tipping to left and right, fingers and thumbs clearly outlined.

"Oh, Max, those are in . . ." Emily felt in her

44

back pocket. "Darn, I didn't bring it. Katie's journal. They're in there, the hands. Just like that, positioned just like that. Oh, I should have it." She stood up, patting all her pockets.

"I'll go get it," said Max. "Where is it? Your pack?"

"Yeah, right-side pocket. Thanks, Max." He disappeared around the edge of the wall and I heard the chink of rock as he dropped down the cliff.

Emily watched him go, then turned and gave me a high five. "This is so great. We found something, first morning."

"What does this mean?"

"Just that Katie was here. It's not a huge deal, because there are a lot of hands in a lot of places, so she could have gotten the idea from other people. But it's a start." She put her hand on the rock next to the old hands, not touching them, but near enough to measure. "They had little hands. Oh, this is exciting. Aren't you glad you're here? I'm glad you're here. You and Max. Even Jenny." She jigged a little. "Dr. Evans will be so impressed."

"Who's that?"

"Women's studies professor. She's in

anthropology and a Hisatsinom specialist. I met Max in her intro to anthro class."

"Intro to anthro." I love all those college abbreviations that sound so casual and knowledgeable. "Max seems nice."

"He's a total sweetheart."

"Are you going with him?"

"Oh, no." Emily bent down again and lifted up little pieces of pottery, felt them carefully, put them back down exactly where she'd found them. "No. Me and Max? That's funny."

"Why?"

"Well, he's three years younger than me for one. And . . . he's just not my type."

"So why'd he come?"

"He loves to climb and we're friends." She sat back on her heels and looked up at me. "That's one of the really nice things about leaving high school, Mira. You can have males as friends without everything getting complicated. It's real comfortable, not a big contest all the time."

A big contest. I knew that's what dating was for Jenny. A major military campaign. Which was why I had avoided the whole idea of getting involved with boys. Too much hysteria, too

much time wasted. But having someone like Max for a friend didn't sound so bad.

"I wonder if I can get a picture in here." Emily began to fiddle with the gadgets. When Max came back in she just grunted and told him to hang on a minute. So he and I took the journal out into the sunshine to find the page with the handprints. Several pages had hands on them, all close, but none exactly right. Then . . .

"There. That's it."

"A Ladder of Hands," Katie had written below it. "It looks like a ladder, doesn't it?"

"Yeah, she's got one . . . two . . . twelve hands? How many inside?"

I ducked into the shadow of the hut again. I counted twelve. Emily came out and hugged us both.

"She was here. Proof positive!" She waved the journal and then took a picture of Max and me holding it between us. When she went back inside to finish her shots, Max said he thought he'd climb the cliff above us. Once he'd disappeared, I sat down outside the hut, my back to one of its walls, and looked out into the morning air around me.

I was curious how long it had taken Katie to

draw the hands. As she sketched, did she wonder whether it was the hand of a hunter, a basket-maker, a storyteller?

And what made the people climb up here with pots of paint in the first place? Maybe it was one person, tracing her own hand and then drawing it again and again, smaller and larger, filling in with color, just like we used to do in elementary school. Suddenly I could see myself standing there, with pigtails, untied Keds, and paint on my hands. A little ghost of myself, feeling all proud to see my handprint hanging on the wall along with the hands of all my friends. Not so different from these people from so long ago, after all.

CHAPTER
4

TO THE LEFT OF THE TRAIL, the cliff rose in waves. It curled above us into the blue sky. I shaded my eyes with the back of my hand and looked deep into the rocks, into the shadows, refusing to blink against the sun's glare and trying to ignore the sweat that crept down the small of my back and the side of my cheek.

We'd been walking down Butler Canyon all morning. The map said it would be a four-hour hike and our time at the storehouse and breaking camp had given us a late start.

Emily said to look for signs of more structures. "You have to really look, Dr. Evans said,

but pretty soon you'll find them everywhere. Something too fixed, too . . ."

"There!" I yelled. "Up there."

Max and Emily looked where I pointed, sighting down my arm to the bright cliff face across the trail.

"It's a house."

"It's a tower."

"I say house."

"I say *who cares?*" Jenny had found the one spot of shade and was waiting in it, fanning herself with her hat, looking very bored. "Let's go."

I pushed past her, ready to find more ruins, because I loved that moment of seeing a building spring out of the cliff at me, like one of the 3-D posters everyone at school was crazy about. I heard her behind me, singing a little tune as she walked, a breathy, formless tune, not a happy tune, more angry than anything.

I turned in the trail. "They coming?"

She took off her headphones and I repeated the question.

"No, they're still arguing. What's the difference? It's *all* old."

Jenny was still all piss and moan, still not awake or into "this hiking business" she kept

muttering about, but even though I set a steady pace, she kept up with me. When I finally stopped to check something that turned out to be just a pile of rocks, she asked for my canteen and took a long gulp. When she started to take another, I took it from her and screwed the lid back on. "There isn't much left. Wait until lunch."

"Slave driver," she muttered and dropped her hand. "I'm hot. And this damn pack is— What are you looking at?"

I pointed across the canyon where a raven was dancing with her shadow along the cliff wall. She dipped and soared and coasted on the air and for a moment I sailed with her.

"You're crazy. It's just a bird." She fanned herself with her hat. Her hair wisped around her face and the front of her T-shirt was soaked with sweat. "Emily is really getting on my nerves. Miss Perfect, Miss Got-It-All-Together. And the way she goes on about Mom. God, you'd think she'd realize we don't want to hear about how *great* 'Aunt Joan' is all the time."

She pushed back her hair. "People who live in the past like that make me tired. Their personal past, I mean." She waved her hand at the

canyon around us, casually including it in her world. "This stuff is OK, I guess, if you like that sort of thing."

"Sometimes, though, it's fun to remember who you were," I said.

"What are you talking about?"

"The little ghost of yourself. I think sometimes it still lives inside me and that even when I'm old, that little ghost will still be there, still half alive." I told her about the handprints lining the hallway of Polk School. She remembered them, too, and even though she said I was *very* strange and that this place was obviously getting to me, she actually laughed.

"God, I'm glad I'm not that age anymore," she said. "Everything was so dumb."

We started down the trail. "What age would you be if you could?" I asked her.

"I want to be twenty-three, on my own, rich, famous, and away from here."

"*Here* here or . . ."

"Utah. Parents. High school. Don't take it personally, little Mira. You can come with me."

"Don't call me little Mira." I walked a little faster.

"So how's Max?" she called to me. I stopped

in the trail and turned around and looked at her.

"What?"

She patted my cheek. "How's Max? Any good?"

"You're disgusting."

She gave me a look, then walked past me, singing *Mi-ra and Ma-aax,* in that teasing tune that also reminded me of grade school.

As I headed up the trail after my sister, I focused on food. I was hungry. The oatmeal and cocoa and juice hadn't lasted long in my stomach, so I dreamed: a rare burger, fries, and a giant Coke. A tuna-fish sandwich, rich with mayo, and a pile of ranch potato chips. A dish of Ben and Jerry's anything chocolate. Fourteen of my own chocolate-chip cookies.

OK, so the best I had to look forward to was beef strips, watery Gatorade, and warm cheese. It was still food. Dad is always warning me about my eating, saying it will catch up with me. But I figure as long as I keep running, I don't have to worry.

Behind me, I heard Emily call my name, so I called to Jenny, and we waited until Emily and Max caught up. Emily said we were stopping

at a creek at the mouth of a draw just ahead.

"Thank God," said Jenny. "I thought we were going to walk all day. I'm dying."

At the creek she immediately dropped her pack, found the one good rock, stripped off her boots and socks, and dangled her feet in the water. Emily told her she was lazy, but she just nodded to the sound from her tape, her hair falling around her face.

Max began to gather up pots, bottles, and some bright green tubes. When I drifted over, trying to get a hint about lunch, he asked me if I wanted to help him filter water.

"Is that what all that is for?" I asked.

"Yeah, we'll go upstream a ways. Find some clear water." He handed me the pots. "Don't want to get sick."

"What kind of sick?"

"You can get something called giardia. Real nasty. Don't ask what it does to you."

"You ever have it?"

"Yes. I wanted to die."

We didn't have to go far until we found a little waterfall pouring over a lip of rock. We filled and filtered five bottles, not talking much above the chatter of the falls. While I did the last

one, he climbed the trail, then came back to say he'd found a great swimming hole.

"Just up a ways. Think your sister would be interested?"

"Don't know." I shrugged. "She likes to swim but she's kind of in a fussy mood today."

"Today?" He gave a twist to the word so I knew he'd got her figured.

But he'd asked about her, so he, like every other male who ever saw her, must have fallen for her blond hair, her beautiful face, and her glitter. Of course he'd ask about her. He wasn't interested in seeing *me* in a wet T-shirt. I didn't care. I really didn't.

Lunch was cheese and crackers, Gatorade, no-melt chocolate bars. Not exactly delicious, but I *was* hungry. We all flopped then for about half an hour, and as I lay, I watched the trees move against the sky, which seemed bluer than the one at home, while I collected wads of white cotton from the cottonwoods. Katie might have spent a morning right here, playing hooky from her chores, pretending she didn't have a care in the world.

When Max mentioned a swim, Jenny

immediately said, "Swim? I didn't bring a suit. Why didn't anyone say anything about swimming?"

"Just swim in your shirt and shorts," said Emily. "It is not a crisis, Jenny."

But she still fussed and fumed and Emily, Max, and I headed upstream while she was braiding her hair and finding the right T-shirt.

It felt so good to walk without the pack on my back that I swung my arms and danced a little to get the full good out of the feeling. This was how the Hisatsis had moved up and down these trails, after all. They'd managed to get along without loads of stuff. I pretended to be a Hisatsis, trying to walk without making a sound, with all my senses alert. Emily, with her short blond hair and compact figure, looked like a Dutch girl who'd gotten lost. But long, tall Max with his long, dark hair down his back could have been a Hisatsis warrior.

The pool wasn't large but was perfectly round, a blue drop surrounded by a circle of red rock, then a band of bright green willows, then more red rock, and finally the sky, which was a blue I didn't have a word for.

"Incredible," sighed Emily. "Let's forget the project and stay here."

Max stepped to the edge of the pool, pulled off his shoes and shirt, and slipped into the water. He swam all around it, disappearing into the deep at times, then got out on the other side and climbed up a ledge that hung out over the water. He called down to us, "It's deep."

He lifted his arms, rose to his tiptoes, and dove into the pool, a clean, neat dive, almost no splash. He looked good doing it: not "buff" as guys say about each other but that tight, clean look I had noticed on swimmers and runners at school, the ones who take care of their bodies so they can use them, not just admire them.

"Hey, looking good there, Max," called Emily and soon she and I hit the water, too, our dives as good as Max's, I thought. The water, warm on top, colder as it got deeper, felt silky on my hot skin. Never had a swim felt so good.

Jenny got there finally and sat dabbling her feet and splashing water on all of us. I splashed her back, so she climbed up on the ledge, where she flung out her towel, put on her headphones, and lay down.

"You wearing sunscreen?" Emily called to her.

"She can't hear you," I said.

"She'll fry up there. All that blond skin. Doesn't she have more sense?"

"She's OK."

"Don't be dumb. If she got a bad burn, she could get really sick." Emily climbed out of the pool and carried a bottle of sunscreen up to Jenny, who looked annoyed. I didn't pay attention to their conversation, just lazed around the pool on my back, soaking up the cool, the sun, the wet, the good feeling of swimming and using muscles different from the ones I used to carry my pack.

Max dived again, several times, and Jenny got up on her elbows to watch him. Then he started a water fight with me. Surprised at first, I fought back, and soon we were dunking each other and splashing, grabbing ankles and wrists under the water. Once I got a handful of his hair; once he lifted me clear out of the water and tossed me to the other side of the pool. I couldn't breathe for laughing and for that half fear of drowning that deep water always holds for me. Emily sat on a rock, calling encouragement and warnings to me.

I was clinging to the side, trying to get a breath, when I saw Jenny get up and walk to the edge of the pool. She reached up and loosened

her hair from its braid, then arched up on her toes, arms straight out in front of her, and pulled a perfect ten dive. We didn't move, just waited for her to surface. She came up shaking her head, laughing, sending bubbles spraying out around her. She thrashed in the water, almost spinning, spraying her hair out around her, sinking in the water, shooting up to the surface.

Max pulled himself out of the water, almost vaulted, and stood in the sun flipping water off his arms and legs. And Emily got out, too, shaking the water out of her hair.

"We'd better get going," she said.

"I just got in the water!" Jenny yelled.

"Your problem. We've got miles to go."

Jenny rolled onto her back and gave Emily a long look. Then she shot one last time out of the water and swam for the edge. She looked good swimming. She looked good doing anything.

I knew everyone thought she was a pain. Emily seemed barely to tolerate her. But, oh, to look the way Jenny looked, to move the way her muscles and bones and skin moved, the way she seemed to part air, to take on light. She occupied her body so well.

CHAPTER
5

OUR SPOT BY THE STREAM looked as if we'd been there a week instead of an hour. Jenny, naturally, hadn't done a very good job of cleanup. The remains of lunch lay around, along with drying socks and bandannas and water bottles and dropped packs. Emily's mouth got tighter. It didn't help that Jenny came down the trail after all of us, looking like a princess, head high in the sun, shoulders proud, padding along as though she owned the trail and the world. As if she'd never in her life done a thing wrong or annoyed a single person.

Then we had to wait while she gathered her

stuff. She couldn't find her dark glasses and wouldn't leave them, even though she had an extra pair, because they were *special* ones, and so we stood around while she went through her pack another time. Finally Emily shrugged out of her pack and went to help her.

"No, let me do it." Jenny pushed her hands away.

Emily turned and looked at Max and me. "Miranda and Max, you go ahead. We'll catch up."

We knew she meant it, so we did as she said, but ten feet away we heard Emily begin and both of us turned to watch. Not exactly polite, but who cared?

Jenny was still pawing through her pack, her bracelets clattering, and Emily stood practically on top of her, hands on her hips. She was listing Jenny's sins: the bad packing job, her late start this morning, her reluctance to work, her lack of initiative, her jump into the pool on top of everyone, the non-cleanup from lunch.

Jenny didn't answer. If you didn't know Jenny, you might think she wasn't listening, or that she knew Emily was right, or that she didn't know what to say, but I knew that Jenny was getting mad.

When Emily finally stopped talking, Jenny sat back on her heels. "You're right," she said. "I *am* a failure. I can't pack a backpack; I don't use the right sunscreen; I obviously wouldn't last a minute living in the wilderness by myself. And, Emily, I don't know how you stand me, because you are so *perfectly* perfect." She stood up and hoisted her backpack onto her shoulders and tightened the belt around her waist. Then she turned toward Emily. "But, you know what, cousin, dear?"

None of us had moved, least of all Emily.

"It's just too bad you can't leave me the hell alone and get your own life. Obviously you need one." She waited just the right beat, then swished past Emily, past Max and then me. I could have sworn she left a little puff of dust in the trail.

Dad has said that even when Jenny was a baby she was constantly asking the world *Why?* or *Why not?* He'd look at her over his glasses and say, "You're not an easy child to parent." And she'd say, "So put me up for adoption."

I don't ask as many questions as Jenny does, but I listen better. I have always wanted to be more like my sister, to have that flair, but I have

also always known it wouldn't happen. I am the quiet one whose absence teachers don't always notice. Jenny's absence leaves a hole in the atmosphere.

I wondered about Katie. Had she been one of the quiet ones? Or had she blazed off to live by herself, leaving everyone missing her? She seemed to know her own mind and she always took the steep and rocky path. She could have lived in town and made money as a seamstress or something. She could have had a regular easy life. She didn't have to live all alone and be different from everyone else and get odd.

Of course, if she hadn't, we wouldn't be following her path a hundred years later. Maybe you have to be a bit weird to be a pioneer. At anything.

I felt a little down as I walked behind Max. The afternoon seemed just a chore to get through. I just walked, put my head down and one foot in front of the other, ignored the heat and the weight of the pack on my back, and counted the frogs that jumped up in front of me.

We'd gone a ways, taken a canteen break, stopped to check out a wall that wasn't a big deal, then gone another stretch when I saw Max

stop ahead of me and heard him talking. I couldn't see Jenny but heard her voice from off to the side.

"Hey, Em," Max shouted. "Jenny found something."

Emily made a sound, one I couldn't decipher, and Max waved his arms and told us to hurry.

Jenny's pack lay on the side of the trail, and she was crouched up a slope under an overhang, her back to us.

"What is it?" Emily called to her, but Jenny just looked over her shoulder and motioned for us to come up. When we did, she still didn't speak, just pointed to the wall in front of her and the lines of drawings that curled up and around its curve: a line of feet like "The Ladder of Hands" and off to the side, a line of animal paws.

"What are those?" I asked. "They look like big cat feet."

"Mountain lion," said Max.

"Are you sure?" asked Emily.

"Yeah, I've seen them up in the Tetons. Those are mountain lion tracks."

"How wild," I said, and when Max said, "Yup," we all laughed.

"How'd you find it?" he asked.

"I was looking. Like Emily said to do. I saw the paws first and then the feet. Not a big deal." She didn't look at us as she spoke, but when Emily said, "Congratulations," they did glance at each other.

"Did Katie draw the paws?" I asked.

"I don't remember them. Let's check." Emily pulled out the journal and flipped pages, found the feet and up in the corner, one paw, very small and without much detail.

"Hmmmm," said Emily, "looks like she ran out of time on this one. Maybe she meant to come back. But it's here." She patted the book. "Oh, this is exciting. What a find. Thank you, Jenny." It looked like it hurt her a little to say that.

"Looks like those charts the gym teachers always drag out to teach us the two-step." Jenny tried a little smile.

"No, it's like when Dad put in the patio in the backyard and we all put our footprints in it. Even the dogs and cats. Remember, Jenny?"

"Yes, and you put your doll's foot in it, too."

As we stood around admiring Jenny's find and eating Max's homemade gorp, the kind with raisins and M & M's and peanuts, I felt the

afternoon brighten, especially when I saw Jenny's face. She was smiling: not her I'm-planning-something smile, or you're-really-getting-to-me smile, or I-like-the-way-that-guy-moves smile, but just a smile. She'd even taken off her headphones. I could see Katie, kneeling here, sketching quickly, thinking about mountain lions and how one could be right around the corner and about how those big paws . . .

"Hey, are there still mountain lions around here?" I asked.

Seeing those big paws made my day. My brightened mood lasted through the rest of the hike, while we set up camp at the mouth of another small canyon that Emily said we'd explore the next day, while we fixed dinner with everyone helping, and while we ate with everyone complaining cheerfully and describing favorite meals in glorious detail.

Jenny started in on school lunch, then school in general: dumb classes she'd had, teachers she liked, hated, laughed at, tolerated.

"God, I can't wait to graduate," she sighed. "To get out of there. People who say high-school years are the best must have really sorry lives."

"Well, I had fun in high school," said Emily.

"It wasn't all wonderful, but it wasn't terrible either."

Jenny just looked at Emily and then smiled into the distance. Max made a sound as he leaned over to fiddle with the stove.

"I'll never say that," said Jenny. "And I'll never look back."

"You plan on coming to the U of U?" asked Emily.

"No! I'm leaving Utah." Jenny stretched her legs and scooped a forkful of chicken noodle something into her mouth. "Maybe I'll go to Boulder or San Diego. A good party school." She turned to look at Max. "Any suggestions?"

"For what? A party school?"

She nodded.

"You're asking *me?*"

"Well, maybe you could tell me which schools you definitely wanted to avoid," Jenny said, not smiling a bit.

"I don't know," said Max. "I just wanted a place where I could spend a lot of time outdoors, preferably in the mountains. I guess I didn't think much about anything else."

"What are you going to do when you graduate?"

"Forestry."

Jenny nodded. "Why did I have to ask! What about you, Emily?"

"I'd like to run a women's center someplace. Combine it with history maybe. This trip has really got me thinking about stuff like that. It's fascinating."

"Oh, you're all so serious," said Jenny as she scraped up the last of her food. "Don't you want to see the world? Dance naked on the Greek beaches? Get drunk in Paris with some beautiful man? Climb the pyramids?"

"You sound like a romance novel," said Emily, getting up and collecting plates and forks.

Jenny watched her for a minute and then smiled. "What's the most outrageous thing you could think of doing? Come on, the most out of character, most wild, most fantastic secret thing you'd like to do. You first, Emily."

"I don't have to do this."

"Of course not. But then we'll wonder why you wouldn't."

We all laughed. A little nervously.

"My most secret fantasy?"

"And most out of character."

"Well, I guess it would have to be the coat."
She poured soap and hot water from the pot

into her dish and began to wash the utensils. "I'd like to have a full-length Russian sable coat."

Jenny looked at her. "You're kidding," she said. "Is that really the best you can do?"

"Look, wearing a fur coat is a major sin these days, you know."

"Yeah, but, isn't there something more . . . daring?"

"I said I didn't want to do this." Emily put the pot back on the stove. "That's all I'm going to say." She didn't sit down again, but continued to fuss with stuff in her bag.

"OK, Mira. See if you can top Emily." Jenny elbowed me. "Try real hard."

"I want to run in the St. George marathon."

Jenny shook her head. "Not out of character."

"OK, I'd like to be an Ogden High Tigerette. Just for one day. Just to know what it would feel like to be able to dance like that." I didn't say that I'd like to see what I looked like in one of their skintight, black, spangly lace outfits. Or to know that every guy and some of the girls in the crowd were thinking about my body.

Jenny let out a disgusted sound. "What a group. When you say *fantasy* most people think

of something a little spicier than fur coats and Tigerettes. Don't either of you ever have real fantasies, like about men?"

I hoped I wasn't blushing, because I did have those dreams, but Emily said, loud enough for us to be sure to hear, "Apparently not as often as you do."

"Well, excuse me for being normal. What about you, Max?"

"I'd like to make it with three knockout women on the fifty-yard line during the halftime show at the BYU/U of U game," Max said without a pause. He smiled at Jenny. "I'm sorry if that seems to leave you out, but if you wanted to watch, I could buy you a ticket."

I realized that my mouth was hanging open when I looked at Jenny. Her eyes and her mouth were *both* wide open, and she'd dropped her cup at her feet.

"Excuse me?" she finally said.

"You asked me," said Max, and he stood up and got a bag of coffee out of his pack. "You guys want some of this? It's decaf."

Nobody said anything, so he measured some for himself, but then Jenny picked up her cup and held it out to him. I sat, looking at my hands.

I felt hot and a little confused. Should I laugh or just ignore what Max had said? *No one* had ever even hinted that Jenny wasn't the best-looking thing around, and here he'd done it so well, so . . . nicely. And then the thought of him "making it" with someone . . . anyone . . . made me even hotter and more confused. His body was right in front of me as he poured hot water into Jenny's cup, and I could see his tight, brown arm and his dusty boots and his long legs and his long, straight black hair falling over his collar.

I stood up quickly and filled my cup with water. Cold.

Emily came back to the circle then and made herself some tea. Jenny looked around at everyone and said brightly, "So, guys, you want to hear my fantasy?"

"No!" said Emily.

"Kidding! Just kidding. I couldn't top Max anyway." She lifted her cup to him, but Max shook his head.

"No, this is a toast to your feet."

"My feet?"

"The ones you found today, both human and feline."

I picked up my empty cup and Jenny poured

a little coffee in it and we all stood and raised our cups and repeated after Max, "To the feet!"

"And to Katie Weston," I said. "Without her we wouldn't know about the feet or the paws or any of this." I swept the night with my free hand.

"Yeah, what a woman *she* must have been," said Max, and he looked at me.

"She must have had fantasies," I said. "That's why she came down here over and over again, why she lived out here in the first place. I don't think she was crazy. She was just different and brave enough to do what she wanted to do."

"Sounds like you're getting inside her head, Miranda," said Emily.

"Are we writing your paper for you, Em?" Max raised his cup again.

"Hey, go ahead. Might be good for some of you. At least Katie didn't spend her time worrying about her sex life." She glanced at Jenny. "She got out and *did* things."

Jenny looked at her across the fire. "Oh, come on, Emily. A person can think about sex *and* be a productive member of society, can't she?" Emily just stared into the flame, and I heard Jenny mutter, very low, "Try it. You might like it."

We were all still standing now, the lantern lighting our faces from below, throwing shadows in strange places. Behind us, the darkness piled up to the cliffs that soared up into the stars.

We looked like four ancient spirits, I thought: Jenny, the goddess of laughter and, yes, sex; Emily, the wise one who kept us all straight; Max . . . Apollo? God of beautiful young men? He looked the part.

Me? I had no idea.

Behind one cliff off to the side, the sky brightened. I pointed to it. "Look, the moon's coming up." Maybe I could be the moon goddess.

"Almost full." Max turned off the lantern.

"Incredible."

"What a place. You can feel . . ."

"Darkness."

"Magic."

"My feet hurting."

"Let's hit the bags. Stay tuned for more magic tomorrow," said Emily, and we clicked on our flashlights and turned away to get ready for bed.

As the day caught up with me, the dinner warm in my stomach, the ache in my legs, the warmth

of my sweatshirt, the long miles behind us, I began to drop away. Sleep wrapped around me, melted around me like chocolate, slow and warm and dark. I thought of Katie and wondered if she'd ever slept down here, if she ever saw the moon, if her husband had been as incredibly sexy as Max was. I made a mound of my clothes for a pillow and let it all go. My last thought was of his blue-black hair.

CHAPTER
6

WHEN I WAS LITTLE I thought that the darkness was a thick blanket that the sun pulled behind it when it went to bed. In the morning the sun pushed off its blanket just like I kicked off my comforter. I had never heard an explanation I liked better. All the thick, rich darkness had to go somewhere to uncover this pale, thin light.

On our second day in the canyon, cotton-wood leaves shivered above me as light crept up the canyon walls across from our camp. The sun kicked off its blanket early down here. I lay quiet for a time, feeling the hollows and bumps of the ground, sensing energy moving through

me. The world lay open above—no ceiling, no roof, just pale green leaves and pure sky all the way to the fading stars.

I took a deep breath and felt a moment of dizziness, then energy that got me out of my bag and up in what felt like one movement. I didn't stop to look around, to see who was up or still down. I just sailed into my shoes and clothes and took off up the trail, to see what lay around me. We hadn't looked around much last night since we'd made camp just before dark, so I had it all in front of me to discover.

I walked, loosening my body, concentrating on breathing in rhythm with my footsteps. I loved being able to tilt my head back to look at the sky, with no pack frame in my way. Amazing to even notice a little thing like being able to tilt my head back, something I wouldn't have thought about back home. Life seemed both simpler and much more complicated here in the canyon.

No clouds. One jet trail off to the side. Noisy birds. Then I started up the little draw that opened out a few yards above our campsite. It looked dark, the sun only hitting the walls high up. No birds sang here, and quiet oozed down

from overhead. The ground was rockier and I had to look at my feet. I moved out and around a rockfall that jutted into the path, then stopped to decide which way to go next. The trail ahead lightened as the sun hit the wall in front of me. I stretched, twisting my body at the waist, first to the right, then the left. And there off to my left, on the wall over my head, I saw her. A dark figure, towering above me, seeming almost to bend into the air above me. I didn't move for a minute, just looked and waited . . . to figure it out, to see it all, to breathe steadily enough to think.

I leaned against a rock and took time to look. The figure looked like a woman, wearing a dress with wide shoulders and lines like lightning bolts zigzagging down the front. She had a square head, blank circles for eyes. She wore earrings.

"Holy cow, lady," I whispered. "You're beautiful." She filled the cliff wall, coming more and more clear as sunshine filtered into the canyon. Her feet were turned as if she was walking up the gulch away from me. And her elbows were crooked and . . . there was someone else . . .

Behind me.

"Hey."

I jumped. It was Max.

"Crap, you scared me."

"Sorry." He leaned over to tighten his shoe-laces. "I followed you. You were up and out like a shot." He straightened. "What are you doing?"

"Look." I swept my arm up at the woman.

He gasped. "Wow. What is . . . It's a fig—a person. Oh, man, amazing!"

"It's a woman. See the dress? And the ear-rings? And maybe even a necklace. See those lines around her neck?"

Max grinned at me. "You're really into this, aren't you?" He leaned against the rock beside me, so close I could feel the heat from his arm on mine. "Hey, looks like she's dancing."

Her elbows, bent so oddly, did look as if she danced to some silent music.

"What's that behind her?" Max stood up and moved closer to the wall. "There's another . . . look, it's a little figure. A kid."

Now I could see clearly what I thought I had seen before, another figure beside her, smaller, much lighter and harder to see, shaped like her.

"They're holding hands," I said.

Now the big figure didn't seem so much to

be dancing as hurrying, with her child clinging to her right hand. I thought of all the times I'd followed my mother before she left us, my mother, who was always hurrying, always with too much to do, arms and hands full, and me, trying to cling to her around cameras and papers.

"A Hisatsis mother," I whispered.

"Hisatsi*nom* . . ."

I repeated it with him. "Hisatsinom. She's in a hurry—she can't wait for the kid to catch up."

"What's she got to do in such a hurry? Why doesn't she slow down and look around her?"

"Moms are always in a hurry. Her daughter painted this, because she had to hold on to her mother with all her strength or she'd get left behind."

"That's kind of sad." Max came back to lean beside me against the warm rock. "It's nicer to think they're dancing."

I shook myself. Remembering the little ghost of myself, clinging to my mother, made me feel cold, sadder than this bright morning should allow. "I don't know." I looked back at the figures. "They're . . . I feel something from her, something . . ."

Max nodded. "Yeah," he said quietly, then he tapped my arm, so lightly I almost didn't feel it. "Hey, how about some breakfast? Race you!"

We ran single file, me first, him behind, not a race but an easy run out of the dark gulch into the warm sun at our camp, where juice and granola waited.

After breakfast we all trekked up to the woman, where Jenny and Emily gasped and pointed, exclaimed over her jewelry and her dress; her child; her wide, staring eyes.

"Fantastic," said Emily. "This is 'Walking Woman.'" She showed us the drawing in the journal, a detailed, careful drawing. "She got it all, the earrings . . . what's that?" She pointed to arching lines coming out of the head of Katie's drawing. "Can you see anything like that up there?"

We all squinted, then Max said he'd climb up and look.

"You can't climb up there," said Jenny.

"I can get closer. See that rockfall at the base? I can get on top and maybe see."

He started up the loose rocks. "Any excuse to climb, he'll find it," said Emily. "He's obsessed."

Jenny and I sat down with our backs against the boulder and looked at the woman. When I told her what Max and I had thought about her, the hurrying and the dancing, Jenny laughed and said she remembered how our mother used to move at top speed.

"Even doing the dishes it was *whoosh, whoosh*—get it done, don't waste a movement or a moment." Jenny shook her head. "I always felt like a slug next to her." She looked up at the woman. "At least this lady took time to put on earrings. More than Joan ever bothered to do." Then Jenny nudged me and leaned forward to clasp her ankles. "You know, I don't think she's dancing." She nodded up at the figures on the wall in front of us. "And she's too stylish for a PTA mom." She rocked back and forth. "I think Walking Woman is a witch."

"A witch? Why?"

She leaned in close to me and pointed up at the figures. "See how the little kid is kind of holding back, and how the big witch mama is pulling on its little arm? You know, like all the happy families we see in Food King, how the kids are always hanging back and screaming? Only these two aren't headed for the frozen

foods. Big mama is gonna take this kid and sac-rifice it to the *thunder god.*" She sat up and made knife movements at my throat.

I pushed her away. "Get real, Jenny."

"Isn't that a fun idea? Hey, Emily, we've got a new idea," she called over to Emily, who was hunched over her camera and tripod.

Of course, Emily didn't like the idea at all and told Jenny the Hisatsinom hadn't done much human sacrifice.

"What's 'not much'? Seems like even once would be too much."

"Dr. Evans told us about a few cases. But they haven't been proved. Listen, I don't have time to goof off. I need to concentrate on getting some good shots of this, OK?"

Jenny pushed back her hair. "I wouldn't dream of intruding."

"Maybe she's a goddess," I muttered, hating the way this was going, the tension rising again between Jenny and Emily. "Goddess of corn or rain or something." I looked up at the woman again, with her long strides, all confidence and power, like pictures I'd seen of Athena, swoop-ing down from Mount Olympus to help out Odysseus.

Emily didn't hear me and Jenny shook her head. "Nope, I like my idea. Call me morbid." She pushed herself up off the ground. "Well, I'm going to go pack. We all know it takes me longer than those of you who are more organized. And I don't want to hold *anyone* up." She looked pointedly at Emily, who ignored her, so she headed down the trail.

All of the talk was fine, but it didn't fit with what I saw on the wall. This wasn't *supposed to be* something. It *was* something. The figures looked real, individual, as if they had names and histories, as if real people had posed for these very pictures.

I climbed the rock slope toward Max and noticed as I climbed how the wall came alive with other drawings: more hands and feet; circles; little figures like deer or dogs, bugs, birds; long, wavy lines like branches.

Max had found a rock that stood about ten feet away from the cliff wall and had climbed to the top of it.

"Miranda," he called down to me. "She does have antennae coming out of her head, just like Katie showed it. Makes her look like a spacewoman."

Spacewoman, witch. Goddess, mother. Real and powerful here in her gulch, headed up the cliff wall, surrounded by life: her child, animals, plants. I could see why Katie had taken a whole page and probably hours to draw her in every detail. Or maybe she had come here often, maybe every time she came down the gulch she came to visit Walking Woman. Like a visit to friends. Or to her mother. Like seeing your own mother whenever you wanted.

CHAPTER
7

CAN YOU BE STALKED BY A PICTURE?

Can someone who never lived talk to you?

Of course, yes, in stories by Edgar Allan Poe.
Or on *Nightmare Theater*.

But here I was in broad daylight surrounded
by perfectly normal people and I felt I was being
watched and listened to. Not spied on, just observed. And not threatened, but . . . checked on,
tested almost. And so I walked a little straighter
and was careful about where my feet landed. I
stepped over every wandering potato bug and
around the smallest plant growing in the trail.

Crazy? Many people would say so, maybe

even all three of the people I was with, but once I had seen the woman, my way of moving, of breathing, of *being* in this place changed. That woman who sailed along the cliff behind us had lived here, maybe died here, and it was her place. She knew these bugs and plants; she'd watched the moon come up and the sun go down; she'd heard every bird in the canyon sing its morning number. This was her home, and I wanted to be a visitor here, not an intruder.

I have always felt presences where other people see only empty space. When I was really little I had a friend who lived in the bathroom mirror and I discovered that witches lived in my aunt's basement. I saw my dog out by the back fence three weeks after she'd died of distemper.

This felt just like that: both the confidence in what I knew and the sure sense that I shouldn't talk about it. I'd done that before and found out that people very quickly made me feel stupid or a little off my noodle. I just knew what I knew and felt what I felt and tried to be ready for what came next.

So when we found the birth panel, I couldn't look at it right away. This was Walking Woman again, only this time she was in deep trouble.

Emily explained a breech birth, how the baby came out feet first and often died and often killed the mother. This panel showed a figure like Walking Woman, with a tiny figure coming out, obviously feet first, from between her legs. The large figure didn't even have a head, although Emily said it once had had one, but the paint had worn away over time. All of Walking Woman's pride and strength had disappeared; her dance had changed to a stiff, awkward pose. She was hurting.

Everyone else was fascinated, even Jenny, who didn't have any trouble at all looking at it and wondering what it meant. She and Emily tossed around ideas: this showed someone who had died giving birth—no, had survived. Yes, this was a warning—no, this was a sacred birthing spot. No—yes. No—yes.

"Dr. Evans said there are a lot of these birthing panels in other spots," said Emily. "But she didn't mention any other breech births. Look at Katie's drawing." She held out the journal to us. Again Katie had been very careful to draw every finger of both mother and child, to show the other smaller figures in the background and then off to the side, the pair of hands that we

could see above us, far to the right side of the panel, deep in shadow.

Emily pointed them out. "Maybe those belong to the midwife," she said.

"I think it's the signature of the artist," said Max. "Like how Katie always put K.W. at the bottom of hers."

That gave everyone something else to talk about as we stood in the shade and looked at the panel. While they tossed around theories, I knew who the artist was: the same daughter who had drawn her mother one gulch down. Once again she showed her mother, now giving birth. The only question was, why had she painted this painful moment? Was it her own birth? The birth of a brother or sister?

"You're quiet, Miranda. You OK?" asked Emily.

I nodded. I couldn't talk about what I was feeling as I looked up at the figures in front of me.

We ate lunch sitting with our feet in the stream and our backs against a moss-covered boulder. Dried bananas, string cheese, crumbly crackers, no-melt chocolate. We didn't even mention anymore how bad it all tasted. It tasted normal.

Emily said we could take a break here since we'd made good progress that morning once we'd gotten going. We had to make it to the little village by nightfall, and we had plenty of time.

"Great! I need a nap," said Jenny.

Emily stood up. "I think we ought to straighten out our packs before we rest." We all stared up at her. "This is the point in the trip where things start to get messy and stuff gets lost." She stopped then, looking embarrassed. Maybe she realized how much she sounded like a tour guide. "It just makes things easier later on," she said, and then shrugged. "At least that's what I'm going to do before I rest." She looked at Jenny. "You guys do whatever."

Jenny flopped in the shade, scooching her bottom into the dirt. I decided to at least look at my pack and see if it could use straightening. Emily was right. Amazing. After just two days, socks lay uncoiled, shirts wrinkled, little scraps of paper were crammed into corners of the pack, tools jumbled in the wrong place. I sorted, tucked, made the little world of my pack orderly again, as well organized as it had been the first day of the trip.

I looked around. Jenny was asleep, Emily reading. Max gone. I decided to clean my body

as well as my pack. I got my bandanna wet from the canteen and dabbed at my hands and wrists and face. I still felt grimy, even when I pushed my hair back with the damp bandanna, even when I wiped my neck. I felt I was so far past dirty that there was no cure short of burning all my clothes and taking an hour-long shower. I couldn't do either, so I wouldn't worry.

When I went to the stream to rinse out my bandanna, I found Max, sitting on the bank, sorting ropes and little pieces of metal. I watched his hands move through the gear spread out in front of him. All this equipment looked so serious, so professional, so necessary.

I must have been staring, probably with my mouth open, because he noticed. So to cover, I asked, "You going to climb?"

"Yeah. Nothing very ambitious, just up to that ridge."

"You need all that stuff to get up there?" I walked over, squatted down, and touched the rope.

"Not really. I just bring it along in case I need it. No, these old guys carved hand- and footholds in the rock. You just have to find the pattern, and then anyplace they used to go, I can go. I take this along for security."

"Can I go with you?" Had I really said that?

"Sure. Come on."

He took out a piece of paper and a pencil, jotted a note, and left it on his pack. "First rule. Always tell people where you're going so they can send out the Saint Bernard if you get lost."

"Why a Saint Bernard?" I helped him coil up the ropes as we talked.

"Oh, my dad always used to say that. Those are the big dogs with the little kegs of brandy around their necks who rescue lost climbers."

"Is your dad a climber?"

"Used to be. He died last year."

"Oh." I leaned over and tied my shoes tighter, folded over my socks. "I'm sorry."

"Thanks. He was cool." He draped the ropes over his shoulder and tightened his belt. "You want to carry the canteen?" He held it out to me. "No brandy in it. Just purified water."

My stomach galloped along beside me as we took off.

He stopped at the base of the cliff and dropped his coil of rope, making the dust billow around him. He'd pulled his hair back and tied it with a length of cord. He'd turned the sleeves of his blue work shirt above his elbows. He

looked in control, like a man who'd done this a thousand times. I couldn't believe I was going with him, that he wanted me along.

"This is a simple climb." He squinted up at the red swell of rock over our heads. "See the little recesses in the wall?" He pointed in a zigzag pattern up the side of the cliff.

"Yes."

"That's where you want to go. Move slowly, place each hand and foot carefully so you don't get caught with no place to move next."

"What happens if I do get caught?"

"You fall."

"No, really."

"You have to retrace your steps and find a new route. But this will be a cinch if you follow me; do just what I do."

"A cinch. OK, I guess."

It wasn't too awful, really. Once I'd started, the rock seemed to hold me, almost pillow me, as it bulged and curved beneath my sprawled form. The way seemed clear, fairly obvious where to reach next, where to wedge in my toes. I almost felt a rhythm as I swung behind Max. Step, step, pull up, reach out with a hand, step, reach. The sun lay warm on

my back, the rock warm beneath my fingers.

And then, of course, I got cocky, put in too much swing, and one foot slipped out of a crack where I'd wedged it carelessly and I felt a spurt, a wash of terror. I clung to the rock, gasping.

"Take it easy. Don't hurry."

I slowed down, finding an easier rhythm. I reached up along the rock face and felt it slope away below my hand, and then Max reached to pull me up onto the ledge where he was standing. When I finally looked at where I was, I realized at once that not only was I gripping Max's arm with both hands but that I was very close to the edge. I immediately stepped to the back of the opening and sat down until my legs stopped trembling and I could look around.

To my left I saw a wall, crumbled bricks, half gone, about three feet high. Max crouched behind it, hands out to either side, touching the bricks gingerly with his fingertips. I stepped up and looked over the edge and saw he was in a little room, made of two crumbled walls coming out from the cliff and a lower wall almost at the cliff edge.

"Another storehouse?"

"Probably. Look." He held up another miniature corncob. "They sure ate hearty, didn't they?"

"Why did they put stuff so high up?"

"Protection. They could get away from their enemies up here. Throw rocks down on their heads."

I looked out over the canyon below us, polka-dotted with shadows, so peaceful it was hard to imagine anyone being an enemy to the people who lived here. Maybe the enemies wanted the peaceful beauty for themselves.

Max had gone farther down the ledge now, bending as he walked, looking at the ground under his feet, sometimes shining his flashlight on a spot, reaching out to look or bending over a scrap of stone.

I followed him, not daring to look too far to my right to the edge of the rock, but out of the corner of my eye I could see sunlight and the bright green of the valley floor.

"Hey, Mira." He crouched below the rock, pointing his light up over his head. "More stuff." He swept the wall over our heads with the flashlight.

I saw three circles, one inside the other, and two half circles of dots off to the right. The circles had been cut deeply into the rock and when

Max shone his light full on them, they disappeared. Only when he held the light to create shadows could I see them clearly.

"This is a petroglyph. It's carved, not painted like the other stuff we've seen. Those are pictographs."

"How come you know so much?"

"I read up." He shifted to his right, brightening more dots and circles.

"Pictograph. What was the other one?"

"Petroglyph. *Petro* is Greek for 'rock.'"

"What does *glyph* mean?"

He shrugged. "Didn't get that far."

"This is different from all the animals and the woman." I reached out to the wall, but he grabbed my wrist before I could touch the stone.

"Don't touch it!"

"Why not?" His fingers felt dry and warm on my skin.

"The oil in your skin will leave a mark."

"Oh." He let go of my wrist. "Sorry." I didn't look at him.

"Maybe these were counting marks. Like . . ." He beat the flashlight against his palm.

"Corncobs," I said. "Or baskets of corn."

"OK. Maybe . . . seasons, or snowfalls."

"Does it snow down here?"

"Sure."

"Maybe it's babies," I said, thinking of the woman and her baby. "Maybe babies that died."

"Could be." He stood up. "Maybe it was a kid learning to count. Or a guy keeping count of the number of girls he kissed."

"Or guys *she'd* kissed." I said it before I thought how it might sound.

"It could be . . . number of deer they'd seen."

"Or shot."

"Or missed," we said together.

"Or"—he stood back away from the wall, hands on his hips, staring at it—"maybe it was someone ditzing around, bored out of his mind, having fun. Whatever it is, we'll have to tell Emily. She'll be *ecstatic*."

We both nodded and grinned.

I stood up beside him. "I don't like these as much as Walking Woman."

"She really got to you, didn't she?"

I nodded.

"I could tell."

I felt myself blush again. "She just seems so real, so alive and . . . powerful, like she owns that rock, that gulch, this whole place. I've felt her around me all morning." I laughed a little,

to make it all right if he laughed, too, but he didn't.

"I know what you mean. It's an amazing portrait."

"And then to see her in the next one, giving birth, looking all helpless."

"You think it's the same woman?"

I stared at him, ready to say *of course,* when I realized it wasn't *of course,* that nothing said they were the same woman except my imagination.

He tapped the flashlight against his mouth. "A record of one woman's life." He looked at the carvings over our head. "Could be."

"Her daughter drew them."

Now he did look at me. "Really?"

"Yes, and the more I think about it, I think women did them all." I gestured back to the storehouse. "Look, it makes sense. The women ground the corn, didn't they, while the men were out hunting? So they were the ones who spent time up here. So while the women worked, their daughters marked stuff on the walls."

He nodded. "You've thought a lot about this, haven't you?"

"It just came to me since I've been down

here. Seeing the woman put it all together. 'Breech Birth' *had* to be done by a woman. So maybe the other ones, too."

I looked at the wall again and could imagine them here, chatting, laughing, kids running all over, moms telling them to get away from the edge, to leave the corn alone, to watch the babies. All the while, someone was working away at the wall behind them, making designs, leaving a record of what was important to her.

"Hey." I felt his hand on my shoulder. "Where are you?"

I shook my head. "Oh, yeah. I'm here." I put my hand up and closed my fingers around his wrist. I looked at him, brave enough to actually look at his eyes, standing there close enough to see that they weren't really black but deep brown. "It's like . . ."

Sounds from below. "Miranda! Max!"

Max squeezed my shoulder once, then turned away to shout, *What?* out into the canyon.

"Max!"

"What?" He cupped his hands and leaned so far out I almost grabbed on to his belt.

"Come down!"

"It's Emily," he turned back to say. "She's pointing."

He looked up the canyon and I looked, too. A huge black cloud filled the sky.

"Storm!" I could hear Emily shout. "Come down!"

CHAPTER
8

I DIDN'T SEE WHY a storm was such a crisis, but I didn't stop to ask for an explanation. I followed Max to the spot where we'd climbed, then went down ahead of him. We ran back to camp, found Emily and Jenny packing our things, threw the rest of our stuff in our backpacks, and in what seemed like seconds from that moment on the ledge, we were headed down the trail. Emily led, then Max, then Jenny and me.

"What's the big deal?" I asked her. "It's just a storm."

"Emily says we've got to get to cover. Someplace up high."

"Why?"

"Flash flood."

The wind had picked up, coming from behind us, and soon I was struggling to keep my backpack upright, to refasten my canteen so it wouldn't tear off my belt, to hold my hair out of my eyes.

"Why don't we just go back there?" I pointed back the way we'd come. Surely the ledge Max and I had been on was high enough.

Jenny shook her head. "I asked her. She said we had to go on to the village. Don't know why."

The sun disappeared and the wind began to moan.

Max and Emily seemed to be arguing, Max gesturing up the side of the cliff, Emily shaking her head. She turned around and gestured at us to hurry.

"Let's stop here," Jenny yelled.

Emily shook her head and turned back down the trail.

"Max! Make her stop!"

Max ran to catch up with Emily. He took her arm, but she pulled away from him and kept walking. Then he pulled harder and she stopped. They stood, their backs to us, clothes

plastered against their bodies. Emily turned to face us and tried to shout into the wind, then we all crouched down together so we could hear her.

"Max thinks we can climb this rockfall. I want to go on to the village. Storm isn't that bad yet."

"Emily . . ."

"No, it's a little rain."

"It's not the rain. You know that."

"I'm going up!" Jenny shouted.

"Em?" Max cupped his hands again and bent near her. "Wind's high. Let's go."

Jenny was already climbing the slope of rock. I started after her. I heard Emily shouting at Max, but then she started up behind me. This was infinitely worse than the climb with Max just an hour earlier. The pack kept pulling me backward; the wind tore at my clothes and nudged me away from the rock. At first I went so fast that my feet kept slipping, but finally I slowed down and reminded myself to breathe. I was beginning to get scared and knew if I gave in to it, I would be in trouble, so I talked to myself all the way up the slope, breathing, moving, not looking down.

By the time I got to the top and turned to help Emily up, I was shaking. The others shook,

too, and gasped as they staggered under the rock. When I took Emily's hand, her skin felt clammy.

Then it started to rain. First big plops that splatted in the dust and then a torrent of water, slashing across the front of our little shelter. We piled the packs against the wind to give us a little protection, then pulled on sweatshirts and hats and wrapped bandannas around our necks. We crept to the back of the shelter and hunched down, hugging our knees and close to hugging each other. Max sat next to me. I tried to stop shaking so he wouldn't know how scared I was.

"That was close," Jenny said when we could all breathe a little.

"We could have made it," said Emily.

"But why risk it? You're the one who said the word *flood.*"

"Because I'm in charge is why. You lead your own trip, you can decide what to do."

"Oh, forget it." Jenny dropped her head onto her knees.

"How could this cause a flood?" I asked. "There's not that much water."

We all laughed a little at that since we couldn't see across the canyon for the rain.

"It might have rained a lot longer upstream

before the rain reached us. And in these narrow gulches it doesn't take much to build to a flood," said Max.

"Oh," I said, and shivered so hard my teeth chattered.

"But it takes a lot more than this," said Emily.

"But as Jenny said, why risk it? We're here now. Let's drop it." Max bit out the words. Then he moved in a little closer to me.

"Won't everything be all mud?" asked Jenny.

"This is a desert, remember?" said Max. "Everything dries fast. We'll be OK."

"What's the worst that could happen?" Jenny said, and when no one answered, she went on. "We could all die here and no one would find us until next spring when a group of Boy Scouts comes down here and they find our four soggy skeletons and they're so grossed out that they all quit Scouts and they don't get their Eagle Scout thing." Jenny always talks too much when she is scared.

"Skeletons aren't soggy," said Max.

"Whatever," said Jenny. "There was this one guy at school, really cute, *very* smart, Key Club, National Honor, all that. We'd talked a little in calculus, so I decided to ask him to the Accolade.

I did the whole silly asking thing, invited him using algebraic equations. Mr. Duncan helped me work it out. I told everybody about it because I had no idea he'd turn me down."

"But he did?" asked Emily.

"Yes," said Jenny. "And you know why? He had to finish up his Eagle project that very night. A Saturday night and he had to be working on some project about birdhouses up at Snow Basin."

"Maybe that was just an excuse," I said, my teeth still chattering.

"Thanks a lot," said Jenny. "Dumb Scouts, anyway. Serve them right if they found our soggy bodies."

We sat and watched the storm for a while then. It wasn't as wild, but the rain fell steadily and the sky looked very dark above the cliffs.

"It's right over us," said Max. "The center of the storm."

Just then, thunder and lightning cracked together right outside our cave.

"Like I said," Max said.

"Look, everybody, I apologize," said Emily. "I just kind of panicked."

"It's OK," I said. "It was scary."

"And now this lightning," Emily went on. "I've seen pictures of people who got zapped. It's ugly. They have marks up and down . . ."

"My God, Emily, will you shut up? We don't need any medical chat right now." Jenny jammed her elbow into me as she edged away from Emily.

Walking Woman, I thought, protect us.

I looked out into the sheets of rain, not just coming from the sky but now pouring off the cliff over our heads so we seemed to be crouched behind a waterfall. Katie probably had been caught in a storm or two down here. Maybe she'd huddled in this very cave. And the people. This was part of their lives, too, this cold and wet, this fear-filled scramble to a shelter, this noise and flash. Walking Woman would have worried about her child and the people who couldn't climb so fast, about the baskets of corn and the new plants and her daughter who'd gone up another gulch to do a pictograph.

"The old people, the Hisatsinom, they must have prayed during storms, don't you think?" I asked. "To the thunder god, maybe, or the god of the earth."

"Probably," said Max.

"So let's pray," I said. "Can't hurt."

Everybody made embarrassed sounds, mentioned not wanting to be in Sunday school and so forth, but I noticed no one said no.

Emily folded her hands and said, "Dear God, please make it stop. We've got things to do. Thank you very much." She ended with a little laugh.

Max cleared his throat. "God of thunder, you have shown us your power in great splendor. Now move on and drop it on the wasted city of Las Vegas. That's west of here a ways. Shake up those sinners with your heat and light." Max nodded to the storm. "Amen."

"You're not joking, either, Max," said Emily. "I know you."

Jenny shook her hands at the rain. "Stop it! Stop it! Stop it!" Then she shrugged. "No one home. I knew it would be a bad hair day." She flipped at her hair that hung in shreds around her face.

I stood up and went to stand at the edge of the cave. I held out my hands into the rain. "Beautiful rain," I murmured. "How they must have loved it when it came." My hands stung under the sharp drops, but my skin felt soft for

the first time in days. "Light. Smooth." Thinking how long it had been since I took time to feel rain on my skin, I held my hands out into the rain again and as I did, the rain lightened, wavered, and stopped. After a moment I smiled and shouted, "See what I did? It stopped!"

They all got up and came to look out, down to the muddy trail below us, back down the way we'd come, where the clouds had disappeared and we could see the sun.

"Hallelujah!" hollered Max. He put an arm around me and I, giddy with the excitement of the storm and the sure sense that it was what he wanted, put both my arms around his waist. We stood together, a little longer than I had planned, clammy and hot as we were, until Emily pushed us apart.

"Let's go," she said. "I want to get out of here."

CHAPTER
9

WE WAITED TO LEAVE THE CAVE until the rain
had stopped completely and the sun looked free
of the clouds. Then we moved out very carefully,
with Max giving directions. He thought we
should lower the packs instead of going down
with them on our backs, so Emily and I went
first. Jenny watched over the edge and shouted
directions to us until Emily yelled at her to shut
up. Then Max rigged a sling with his ropes and
lowered the packs to us one at a time. Finally
Jenny and Max came down. The whole thing
made my nerves jangle; everything felt slick with
mud, wet, and soft to the touch. I couldn't get a
firm hold anywhere.

When we'd all landed safely, we stood looking at each other and laughing.

"Drowned rat time," I said. "We're a mess."

"Yeah, but the worst didn't happen," said Max.

"Hey, we're not out of here yet." Jenny bent over and shook out her hair, letting it blow in the warm air. We all watched it and her and I couldn't help noticing how much Max noticed. The best I could do was take off his bandanna and shake it dry. My short brown hair wouldn't look half so beautiful in the sunshine. But he'd hugged *me*. And I could still feel his fingers circling my wrist.

Emily for once let some drawings go by. Max and I told her what we'd found, but she shook her head. "No way I'm doing more climbing. I just want to get to the next stop."

We did take time to rearrange our packs and find things that had been stuffed in wrong places in our hurry. We put on dry clothes, hanging the wet stuff on our pack frames. The air felt clear and cool, the sun warm but not the hot of other afternoons. The path was muddy but looked like it was already drying. Puddles of water stood in the trail, and when I bent over one, I saw small swimming creatures.

The sky and the red rock looked clear-edged and clean, just the way the valley and mountains at home look in that first hour after a storm. I filled my lungs with the air, did it again, then stretched. Amazing to think how scared I'd been just a little while ago.

While Jenny played with her hair and Max coiled up his ropes and Emily got out the map and the journal to figure out how far we had to go to the village, I thought about that fear. At first I didn't believe we'd really been in danger, not like Walking Woman and her family would have been, or like Katie was every time she came down here alone. I felt that someone, somehow, would come and bail us out of any trouble we might fall into, as if we could just call 911. I knew it wasn't quite that simple. Then I looked around at the cliffs and the empty trail that went forward and backward from where we stood, the trail we'd been on for three days now without seeing anyone. We were really alone. Sure, if we didn't come out, eventually someone would look for us, but a load of bad stuff could happen to us while we waited.

I had been very smart to be very scared. And as I looked at them being their careful selves, I was glad I was with Max and Emily, who knew

what they were doing and weren't afraid to take the time to do everything right.

Still, I couldn't shake the feeling that we would be all right here only as long as we didn't forget how close to the edge we walked. There was no emergency phone around the corner. The storm had reminded me of that, and our prayers for protection felt real, in spite of our laughter.

After making final adjustments of stuff and handing out a granola bar apiece, Emily got us on the road. The air still felt wonderful; it seemed to carry our voices better so when Jenny started singing, echoes bounced back to us. Her bracelets tinkling, she even danced a little as she walked, a far different Jenny from the one who'd complained all the first afternoon.

Now it seemed as if the world had come down to this: the warm sun washing everything yellow, the weight of the pack on my back, so familiar by now, everything where it needed to be, the bandanna Max had given me around my neck, my shoes laced just tight enough, my canteen at just the right spot on my belt so it didn't get in my way, the waist strap of the pack notched

at just the right spot and riding my hips at the perfect level.

It isn't often that everything in your life is just right. Usually there's something that nags at you. Down here I had time to think about what I was doing and seeing and feeling. Like the rain on my fingers.

Walking Woman had lived here without microwaves and cars and books and beds. She must have had a lot of time to watch the sun, to follow her little child down to the water and watch her play with frogs. Sure, there was all the hard stuff of life that made "Breech Birth" difficult for me to look at, but now, walking through this peaceful afternoon, I let myself forget all that and focus on how clear life lay around me. My mind could concentrate on what lay under my feet and what stretched only as far as I could see.

Up ahead Max suddenly dropped his pack. He climbed a bank of red dirt and ran back and forth along the top of the slope, then dropped back down to the trail, swept up his pack, and was walking again before I caught up with him. Like a big puppy.

I could look at Max for hours, at the way his

dark hair fell around his eyes, at the shy way he smiled, shy but still sexy. He did look good in his jeans, as Jenny said, but I also noticed the straight way he stood, how he hooked his hands in his belt loops, his long legs and arms. At school I wouldn't have dared do more than stare at someone like him, and here I was living with him, watching him act goofy and smiling when he tossed me a wave.

On our walk that afternoon, Emily sent us on several scouting expeditions to check out possible ruins and panels. We found more feet and hands, more circles and dots, and a lot of hunting scenes, people shooting arrows at deer. Katie had several pages of these in her journal. That made Emily happy. Every time she could check a page of the journal off on her list, she chuckled and bragged about how great her paper was going to be. I didn't mind because, by now, I felt that paper was ours as much as hers and I wanted it to be worthy of Katie.

Then I found Kokopelli carved on the side of a rock and Emily went ballistic. She practically jumped on top of me and screamed, "We found it! We found it! Thank you, thank you, thank you, Miranda!" I bent over the faint outline of

the humpbacked man and wondered what made him worth such hysteria.

Then Emily explained that no one had ever found a picture of Kokopelli in this gulch and it was one of the reasons experts thought Katie's drawings were copies of other people's findings.

"So what is Kokopelli?" I asked. "He isn't much to look at." Nothing like Walking Woman, I thought.

"Can't you see what he is, Mira?" asked Jenny. "Look real hard at him. It's pretty obvious."

"What's obvious? He's all bent over and it looks like he's holding a stick or something."

"He's playing a flute." Emily pointed to the line that did look like an instrument of some sort, now that I knew.

"And what else do you see?" asked Jenny. "Look hard."

"Well, there's another line down there." I pointed.

"Not just another line, baby sister. Old Kokopelli isn't just any old flute player. He's a fertility god. That's his penis."

I dropped my hand. "How do you know? You don't know about this stuff, Jenny, so don't make things like that up."

"It's true. Ask Emily."

Emily nodded. "He was a major figure for the Hisatsinom. Most ancient people had someone like him—the Greeks, Egyptians. You find some version of his picture in almost every ancient site."

"And he's big stuff for the tourist trade, too," said Jenny. "That's how I recognized him, from Dad's Sundance catalog. You can buy Kokopelli jewelry and T-shirts and coffee mugs."

"Like that?" I pointed to the figure.

"Sometimes."

I hadn't dared look at Max through all this. I thought I was quite cool about sex, but to have it here, carved on a rock, like someone would write his initials, was another thing entirely.

We waited while Emily made her notations and took a picture of Koko, as Jenny was calling him. Now Emily was unstoppable. She had ticked off almost everything and, for the first time, showed us her list.

"I thought it would just discourage you before," she said. She'd crossed off the feet, "The Ladder of Hands," and the mountain lion paw, the circles Max and I had found, "Walking Woman," and "Breech Birth." And now "Kokopelli."

"We need the turkey tracks and the moons. We *really* need the moons." She closed the journal and held it to her.

Jenny came to stand in front of her and gripped both her shoulders. "Emily, we'll get the moons." She turned and gestured to Max and me. "Won't we? We'll get the moons!"

"Yes! We'll get the moons. We'll get the moons!" We chanted, louder and louder. "The moons! The moons! We'll get the moons!"

Emily looked disgusted and waved her hands at us, but she was laughing. "Oh, you guys."

We kept chanting quite a ways down the gulch and the afternoon wore away without our really noticing. Dark comes very quickly that deep in the earth without the long afterglow we get from the sunsets over the Great Salt Lake. As deep in Katie's Gulch as we were, the sun drops and is gone. Once I tripped; I'd seen Jenny trip several times. When I heard Max tell me to be careful of an overhanging branch, I realized I was having trouble seeing the path. I hollered to Emily that we should slow down, and so we did. We began to hear night sounds, rustles and murmurs from both sides of the path. None of us spoke, just

moved a little closer together on the trail and walked more carefully. It wasn't completely dark but dim and dimming, shadows deepening and broadening.

Finally I heard Emily call back to us. "We're there! Just wait! Just wait!"

Max and I saw it last as we came around the bend in the trail and looked up at the slope in front of us, through the fringe of juniper trees, at the little village.

It looked alive in the evening shadow, sleepy but livable. Nestled under the cliffs, not up in them, the little houses lay just up an easy slope from the creek, three or four layers of houses stacked one on the other. A shaft of the last bit of sunlight fell on the buildings. It was what we in our family always jokingly called a hand-of-God moment.

We dropped our packs under the trees and headed up the slope, past what Emily told us was the garbage dump.

"Archaeologists really love those," she said, pointing to the loose pile of rock and dirt.

"They love garbage?" said Jenny.

"It's the best place to find what people ate." She squatted and ran her hand loosely through

the dirt. Then she held up what looked like a small dark twig and flipped on her flashlight so we could see it. "Look at this. It's the rim of a basket. See the fiber twisted around the edge?" She held up a piece of pottery. "Tons of shards."

"And corncobs." I found three right around my feet.

"Any bones?"

"Not human ones. Maybe some turkey bones. They didn't bury people this close in."

Jenny and Emily huddled over the garbage dump, for the first time on the trip seeming at ease with each other. Maybe Emily's apology had done it, or maybe Jenny had just smoothed things over with her silly stories and songs. Whatever had happened, it was a relief.

Then Max pointed higher up the cliff at another level of houses, twenty, thirty feet above the main group. We could barely see it in the shadows. "Wow," he said, "Now I could . . ."

I gaped at the houses hanging almost in space. "They lived up there? How did they get there?"

"Ladders. Look, there's part of one still hanging there."

Jenny had slumped on a rock behind us.

"Look, I'm kind of hanging here myself. I need my dinner and bath and my comfy bed."

Emily carefully put the piece of the basket on the rock where Jenny perched. "Let's have dinner. Time tomorrow for all this. Remember, we'll be here two nights. Shall we camp down there in the junipers?"

We all moved down under the trees and started stamping the ground.

"Looks good."

"Far enough away from the ghosts."

"I'm hungry."

"For a steak."

"And fries."

"Don't get your hopes up, guys. It's freeze-dried Hawaiian chicken and carrot strips."

Moans.

"But . . . chocolate pudding for dessert."

CHAPTER
10

We set up camp and finished dinner quickly. We had to move carefully in the darkness. Max suggested that we climb up into the little village to watch the moon come up, but when Jenny teased him about having romantic ideas, he got quiet and didn't mention it again. I thought it was a great idea and after we'd cleaned up, I told him I'd like to go with him. I didn't care if I got teased. Jenny and Emily didn't say anything when we headed toward the now gloomy ruins.

We both had good flashlights and used them on the trail and while climbing through the houses. We had to be careful not to step

anywhere but on dirt and rock, to avoid the ruins that looked very fragile. We found a boulder halfway up and Max said we shouldn't go any farther, so we climbed it and settled on its wide smooth top.

"This place reminds me of a playhouse I had when I was little," I said. I felt a little out of breath, not just from the climb. "My mom built it in the backyard and she let me paint it inside. I painted it all white and then put green lightning bolts all over the walls."

"Sounds cool."

"It was. These houses look like playhouses."

"For little people," he said.

"Where'd they keep all their stuff?"

"They didn't have much stuff."

"Just all this." I swept my arm at the cliffs across from us and the night and the stars and the valley at our feet.

"I'd trade."

"Me, too."

Then we sat and watched the darkness below us, the two tiny points of flashlights where Emily and Jenny moved around doing—what? Odd how random their movements seemed from here, although they must have had reasons for

moving as they did. Life turns funny when you get away from it for a while and take a long look back.

"Moon will be up soon," said Max.

"Do you suppose Emily planned this trip during a full moon? It's so perfect."

"Maybe. Knowing her, though, I think she planned it to fit her schedule. She's always got stuff going on. Most organized person I know."

"She's always been that way. Her mother never had to remind *her* to send thank-you notes."

We both laughed.

"Is she like your mom?" he asked.

"She's my dad's niece. But she and my mom are kind of alike."

"Is it hard not having your mom around?"

I shrugged. "Not so much now as it was. It's harder on Jenny. She needs a lot of, you know, attention."

He grunted. "Yeah."

"My dad's great. Usually."

We sat quiet then. It felt comfortable, easy, friendly.

"You know that Kokopelli guy?" he said quietly.

I nodded, then said, "Yes."

"You don't need to be embarrassed about stuff like that. It's just a part of life. Sex, I mean."

"I wasn't embarrassed."

"You should have seen your face."

"Well, I'm just not used to seeing things like that out in broad daylight is all. Besides . . ."

"What?"

"I love the woman so much and 'Breech Birth' really bothers me. So seeing him, so obvious like that, well, it seems kind of . . . sick."

"Oh, no." He straightened up beside me and leaned forward so his face came into the dim light more clearly. He looked very serious. "In that anthro class I took with Emily, we talked about sex a lot. See, those ancient people accepted everything a lot better than we do. Sex and birth and death were just a part of life." He looked right at me. "And these pictures are like celebrations of all that."

"Celebrations? Of something that might have killed her?"

"How do you know it means she died? Maybe it's to mark that she survived, that this was a very special child because it was born that way. Everything doesn't have to be dark. Even death isn't always dark."

I didn't say anything, just tried to put "Breech Birth" and the word *celebration* together.

"But when your dad . . . I mean . . . did you feel that way when *he* died?"

He didn't answer right away, but then he cleared his throat and said, "Not at first. I was really bitter. It didn't make any sense to me."

"How'd he die?"

"Car accident. A real stupid one." He flipped a pebble out into the darkness, an easy flip into the darkness, and I thought about how he must have looked when he heard, his brown eyes turning dark and his long, strong fingers twisting around each other.

He took a long breath. "But then after a while, I began to remember good stuff and I realized that nothing would make any sense if I just stayed unhappy. My mom helped a lot, too. She's a modern Walking Woman. Nothing gets to her for long." He picked up another pebble, but just tossed it from one hand to another. "At least, not so I can see."

As I looked out at the valley in front of us, dark and mysterious, I thought about how hard it would be to lose my dad, how long it would take me to remember the good stuff.

"Your mom must be pretty tough, too. I

mean, you and Jenny aren't exactly cream puffs."

"Thanks." I put my arms around my knees and rocked back and forth on the rock. "I guess you're right. And my mom's OK, too. Even though she's pretty involved in her own life."

"Yeah, well, we've got to let them do their thing or they'll drive us crazy worrying about *us*, right?"

I chuckled. "Right." He leaned against me, just a little. He felt warm and solid. How comfortable it felt to sit in silence beside this friend, this person, this *lovely* male person.

"Just think of them back there in the darkness," he said after a while. "Kokopelli, Mr. Macho, strutting his stuff, even though no one's looking." He nudged me gently.

"And the beautiful dancing woman with her child. Holding on to each other."

Suddenly we were hit with light. "Moon!" we both said together, and straightened up to look across the canyon at the white light streaming down on us.

Soon moonlight washed over everything. The houses and rocks around us and the cliff above sprang into detail in the bone white light. I hugged my knees and watched, leaning against

Max, and without making a big deal about it, he put his arm around me.

Then he stood up and pulled me up, too, then climbed down from the rock, signaling for me to follow. Once on the ground, he put both arms around my waist and waited until I reached up to put my arms on his shoulders. Then we began to dance, there in the moonlight, there with each other.

We didn't say another word, just danced, held hands, and finally, slowly, carefully kissed . . . then kissed again. I felt shot with silver, from the moon, from the dance, from Max.

CHAPTER
11

THE NEXT MORNING I woke up before anyone. It was barely light, but I couldn't sleep anymore. All of yesterday lay tumbled in my mind and flashes of it made me smile and sigh as I tiptoed away from camp, up the stream, trying to move as Walking Woman would. I found a spot where the stream took a little bend and puddled up, deep enough to soak my feet, to get my bandanna wet without trapping sand or polliwogs.

I laid out my clean clothes, the one clean shirt I had saved for last, and my soap and towel, then I stepped out of shoes, shorts, shirt, and underwear, shaking them free of dirt. I stretched

once, then more widely. How good the air felt on my skin, how free I felt without clothes for the first time in days. I shook my hair out, bent over, and shook it again, digging into my scalp with my fingertips. I wet the bandanna and washed my body all over: face, neck, arm, stomach, chest, legs, between fingers and toes. I stretched again, feeling the air warm on my wet skin, easing out all the aches from the night and the walking of the past three days.

As I reached to get my towel, I realized I was smiling. Standing here in a tiny pool, naked and still half dirty, smiling. At no one.

Yes, but last night I had been kissed! By Max!

Last night! I thought about everything we talked about: his father and mother, my mother, Kokopelli and celebration; and everything we did: arms wrapped around each other, the careful first kiss, his hand touching my neck and arm, my hand stroking his long hair, his breath mixing with mine, then his kisses that frightened me because I didn't care what happened next, until he backed away from me and, holding both my hands, looked at me. Without saying anything, we walked down the slope to camp.

I suddenly realized I'd been standing there

stark naked in that stream for quite some time and that Max himself could walk up this trail any moment. I grabbed my shirt off the bank, slipped it on, then eased onto a rock, and dabbled my feet in the water.

I watched the water circle out from my feet. My life at home would seem empty after this trip. Turning on a faucet and getting hot water would almost seem like cheating. Shopping for school clothes would seem like a silly waste of time.

I stood up in the middle of the stream, stretching every way I could, feeling my body and mind tingle, and I turned slowly in the water, feeling it lap around my ankles, feeling the air on my face and neck and hands.

"Help me remember everything," I whispered.

Our plan for the day was to go on up the draw to the kiva. Emily had told us that the kiva was a thing we had to see, and then she explained what it was.

"The Hisatsinom believed their ancestors came from the center of the earth, up through a hole in the ground, a *sipapu*. The kiva is a big underground room, to remind them they came

from under the earth. It's where they had their sacred ceremonies and their clan meetings."

"It's a hole in the ground?" asked Jenny.

"When the kivas were first built, they were covered, with an entrance hole. This one has been rebuilt, it says on the map. Most of them are in pretty bad shape by now." She tapped the map with her pencil. "I can't wait to go down in a kiva. They didn't let women in them in ancient times, so I'm going down there and just show them."

"Show who what?" I asked.

"That there's nothing wrong with women," she said. She didn't answer the *who*.

"That doesn't necessarily mean anything negative," said Max. "There could have been lots of other reasons women didn't go down there."

"Name three."

"I don't know, Emily. I haven't given it much thought, but it doesn't have to be a major put-down."

"Well, I'm going down there for sure. *No one* can keep me out." She stood up and slung on her day pack, looking ready to fight someone. None of us looked interested, so she couldn't do anything but stomp on down the path.

"Well," said Max. "I think I'll stay out of her

way for a while. She's on one of those things of hers."

"We'll protect you, Max," said Jenny.

"Thanks," he said, but he smiled at me. We hadn't talked alone this morning, but he looked glad to see me when I came back from my bath and he sat by me while we ate breakfast.

To me he looked beautiful.

Now headed up the trail for our last full day together, I looked at everything, noticed everything: the tiny yellow flowers by the side of the trail, the cliff swallows swooping and twisting above us, the taste of the juice still in my mouth, the color of the sky that I still didn't have a word for, how long Max's legs were as he walked ahead of me. I'd knotted his bandanna under my hair again and liked the feeling that I was wearing something of his.

We'd left our packs at the village, so I could swing my arms, I could run down the trail after I stopped to look at a frog and everyone got ahead of me, I could dance a little behind everyone else.

What a morning.

After a very short walk, one bend in the trail brought us into a wide valley. The canyon walls

fell away on both sides of us. The cliffs were still high, but for the first time since we'd come into the gulch, they weren't as terribly steep. A person could hike up the fat swoops of stone until she got near the top.

"Perfect Kiva. That's where we're going." Emily pointed at the level of the shelves, as if her finger cut a path across the slick rock. I couldn't see anything that looked human-made in all that brightness and color. It was hot by now, and we took a minute to stand in the shade of a juniper and drink from the canteens.

"It looks like a long way, Emily. Can't we do it later?" asked Jenny. "I think I'm getting a blister." She looked across the valley toward the cliffs. "How far do you think that thing is?"

"Not far. Let me look at your foot." Emily reached into her day pack. "I have some moleskin in here."

"No, it's OK. Thanks anyway. Can we eat up there?"

"Jenny, it's a sacred place," I said.

"So we can't have a snack there? People eat in church all the time." She refastened her canteen and headed out of the shade, waving to us. "Let's go."

We all looked at each other. "Who eats in church?" said Emily. Then she hollered after Jenny, "I thought you wanted to wait." But Jenny didn't stop, so we all followed her out into the light.

She didn't last long in first place. As we passed her, she moaned, "I am baking in this heat."

"Sizzling," said Max.

The walk didn't look far, maybe half a mile, but that half mile was all between hot sun and hot rock. It made us silly.

"I feel like a poached egg."

"Toast."

"Burned toast."

"Broiled chicken, bacon, hot dogs."

"Corn on the cob. *Tiny* corn on the cob."

I felt as if the heat were holding me between sky and rock, turning me from side to side to get a smooth, even brown. After a bit we quieted, panting under the weight of the heat, concentrating on our steps up the folds of rock, across the shiny surface of baked stone.

At first I kept track of our progress up the slope, but after a while I didn't care, just put my feet down until Emily told us we had arrived. I sensed it before she spoke, felt the slope lessen,

felt a sudden coolness edge at the heat. As I rounded the corner, the great shelf of stone that had looked so distant opened before me, as if a giant hand had molded it.

I walked under the shelf, out of the sun into a cool cave, a rose brown dampness enveloping me, wrapping me away from the golden heat. The rock arched over my head like a huge clamshell.

I breathed in the cool air and let my eyes adjust to the dimness. In the shadow at the back of the cave, I saw a small building with one door and a wall about two feet high making a circle in front of the hut.

"Is that the kiva?" asked Jenny. "I thought you said it was underground."

"This is it." Emily pointed inside the circle at a square hole with two poles sticking out of it. "This is the entrance." She swung a leg around the ladder and started down into the kiva.

Jenny peered in after her. "What do you suppose they did down there? Told dirty stories? Looked at *Playboy*? Smoked a little dope?" She swung her leg over the side onto the ladder just as Emily had done. "Well, I want to see what the big deal is. You guys coming?"

"In a minute," said Max. He was bent over

a display of pottery shards and corncobs lying on top of the low wall. "Look at these, Mira." He touched them with his fingertips. "They really knew how to throw a pot."

"Look at the design on that one." I pointed to one painted in bold black lines. "I like the painted ones. They look so modern. Like what we make in ceramics."

"So did the women make these, too?"

"Yeah, sure, why not?"

Just then Jenny's golden head popped up through the kiva hole, followed by her bracelets, arms, legs. "Just a dirty old hole in the ground," she said as she stamped her feet free of the dust. "Not such a big deal. Maybe the women sent the men down there to get rid of them."

"Is Emily down there painting sisterhood signs all over the walls?" asked Max.

"No, she's just sitting there, gazing into space. I think she's putting a curse on all the men who kept the women out." Jenny mopped her face with her sleeve. "I know why the women didn't go down there. It's way boring."

"Well, maybe I'll take a look," said Max.

"Be my guest." Jenny waved at the ladder. "Miranda? You coming?"

"I don't think so. I like it up here."

He disappeared down the hole. I was glad he hadn't asked why I didn't go with him. I wasn't sure why I didn't want to go down the kiva—it just didn't seem right.

"Emily's acting a little weird about this, isn't she?" I said as Jenny paced, peering up at the rosy walls.

"Oh, she's just a fanatic. Being weird is her job. But I'm getting used to her. Just don't let her bug you."

I wanted to laugh at Jenny. Yesterday she was ready to kill Emily. Now she was the expert giving me advice on how to get along with her. My sister!

"Hey, Mira." She flapped her hand at me. "Look!"

"Not another Kokopelli."

"No. Didn't Emily say she needed turkey tracks?"

I got up and went to look over her shoulder. Up the side of a smooth stone that lay against the back of the cave marched what looked like arrows but, when I looked closer, did look like some kind of bird track.

"Big, aren't they?" I said.

We called Emily and she, of course, was ecstatic and gave us both hugs, took pictures, made notations, and made a big deal of crossing turkey tracks off her list.

"Now you're going to tell me they had Thanksgiving dinners, aren't you?" Max said when he climbed out of the kiva to see our discovery.

"We don't know if they ate turkey," Emily said seriously, and we all looked at each other and tried not to laugh. "But they did make clothes out of the feathers. Dr. Evans brought a picture of a turkey robe. Oh, and she told us the saddest story. The robe was made of a kind of hemp net with the feathers wrapped around the net. The net was made into a blanket that was wrapped around a baby. The mummy of a baby." She held up her hand. "No jokes about that, Jenny."

"No, ma'am."

"A mummy of a baby?" I looked at her, wondering if I had heard her right.

Emily nodded. "Dr. Evans had pictures of it. Sweetest little thing. You could see her little hands, and she still had some of her hair and one tooth."

Now no one looked at all like they wanted to make a joke.

"You could tell they really loved that baby, the way they'd wrapped her in that warm robe, put two little bowls in with her for food. Someone found her in a wash and took the pictures before they buried her again."

"A mummy," said Jenny, almost in a sigh.

"It's dry down here. Things keep."

The others all went back down into the kiva again, while I sat on the edge of the cliff with my legs hanging out into the air and thought about the baby, how hard it would have been to keep a baby alive in such a place. How often a mother and father must have had to wrap a baby in a soft turkey robe and put her into the ground. Maybe Walking Woman was dancing because her child had lived long enough to hold her hand and walk beside her.

CHAPTER
12

AND FINALLY THE MOONS. Since Katie had put them on a page right after the turkey tracks that were after Kokopelli, we thought it made sense that they would be near here. Once everyone else had looked at the kiva, and after we'd had our snack, *outside* of the kiva on a shady ledge nearby, we started the search.

"Let's fan out. We may find more that way," said Emily. "But keep within sight of each other."

We did fan out and we did stay in sight of one another, but all we found were more dots and feet and some spirals, which Emily said Dr. Evans had said were symbols for water. They

were nowhere near any water, but they might have marked a water source six hundred years ago.

We exchanged discoveries after two hours of looking. It was high noon and the only shade we found was a tiny patch under a juniper. We pulled out canteens and mopped our bright red faces.

Emily wasn't discouraged. "On a day like this you can understand why these people left here." She had on her lecture voice, one I was used to by now. "You know, these people just disappeared over six hundred years ago. Very mysterious. They left all kinds of stuff—pots, clothes, weapons."

"Maybe they all died of sunstroke," said Jenny, fanning herself with her hat.

"Why did they leave?" asked Max.

"Well, the first theory was that the ancestors of the Navajos drove them out, but the Navajos came about two hundred years after the Hisatsinom left. Then the theory was that disease wiped them out."

I thought of the baby. She'd probably got sick.

"The most plausible one is that they ran out

of water. Getting water must really have been a chore. They had to carry it up and down, either from the canyon floor or the mesa top."

"But we know it rains down here," I said.

"Yes, but that isn't reliable."

"Well, they sure knew how to climb," said Max. "Their paths up and down the cliffs are still perfectly usable."

"But carrying water jugs?" I tried to imagine how they would do that, remembering how hard it was to climb with my pack.

"Well, they vanished," Emily continued, "and left all this. They probably moved south."

"They turned into snowbirds. Moved to Mexico to lounge on the beaches." Jenny yawned. "I'm up for a little lounging myself. Couldn't we take a break?"

"I really want to find the moons. Miranda, Max, you up for a little more looking?"

"I have an idea," I said. "Maybe they are more visible at night."

"Hey," said Jenny, "that's an oxymoron, Mira."

"Listen to the Junior Seminar talk. Miss Onstott would be proud of you." I flipped a handful of water onto her legs and she made a face at

me. "What I mean is that maybe when it gets darker and more shadowy, they'll show up."

"It's far out, Mira, but we can give it a try. We've pretty much done this valley." Emily looked around her and laughed. "What am I saying? We haven't scratched the top layer of this place. But we've tried." She stood up and straightened her clothes. "Let's head back to the village so Sleeping Beauty can have her nap. We'll look around this evening."

We slumped back to camp, walking slowly, like tired turtles, moved our sleeping bags into the shade, and all found a place to stretch out for a while. I like this way of living, getting up early when it was cool, doing work during the morning, and then resting in the afternoon. It made me think of kindergarten again. I was sure the woman would have made her child lie down and rest through hot afternoons and that Katie must have settled under a tree to do her drawings and rest after her long hike in from the ranch.

Even with the hard ground under me and a fly that wouldn't leave me alone, I felt peaceful. Across the stream, Jenny snored lightly. Up the slope in the shade of a boulder, Emily looked

through the journal one more time. And once the other two weren't looking, Max came and sat down under my tree, close enough that our shoulders touched and we could hold hands.

"Max, what do you suppose it was like when they left? Emily said they left all their stuff behind."

"They couldn't carry much with them."

"They must have been so sad."

"Yeah, all leavings are sad." He squeezed my hand.

To leave behind this place, I thought, where they knew all the bushes and trees, how to avoid the sharp stones on the trails, where to find the best food and water. They would have to leave behind the kiva and Kokopelli and Walking Woman. How could they bear to leave? Even if they had to?

This would be our last dinner down here. Oh, we'd meet again, for sure; we might get together to look at pictures and reminisce over burgers and fries. But we wouldn't be in this canyon under this light with these adventures still circling around us. And Max would bring his girlfriend and look embarrassed when he introduced her to me. I would pretend not to care a bit.

After her nap, Jenny said she'd cook and didn't even make a face when Emily told her it was beef stroganoff, green beans amandine, and no-cook applesauce. Emily volunteered to help!

I wandered up toward the village to find a place where we could eat, and Max followed me, muttering about wanting to get up to that second level of houses. But he didn't bring his climbing stuff with him.

Together we explored the houses, wedging ourselves through narrow doors into tiny rooms built against the cliff wall, feeling the deep cool that came from the center of the earth and seeped into our bodies. We ran our fingers over the ceilings blackened with soot from old fires.

"I feel at home here," I said. "Is that weird?"

"No. Look, if you brushed out the floor and put a layer of juniper branches over the roof poles, you'd have a fairly good house," Max said. I looked at him, where he stood with one arm looped over the rock wall and his hat low over his eyes, then around me at the little village. I could almost feel the spirits of the ancient people as they walked down to the creek, as they swept out the dirt floors and ground their corn on the grinding stone.

This might have been the house of a young

man and woman, not much older than Max and me. A wave of such sadness came over me that I had to put my hand out onto the cool rock and make myself breathe.

When I was steady, I held out my hand. "Max."

He turned to look at me.

"Let's find a good place up here to eat our last dinner together."

When we found the perfect rock for outdoor dining, we brushed the dust off it and began setting places for each of us.

"A sprig of sage for Emily. She loves the smell."

Max handed me a wide, flat red rock. "Put the sage on that."

"I'll get some sweet peas for Jenny from the creek."

"And here's a sparkly rock for her. She's kind of a sparkly type."

"You like Jenny? I mean, how she looks?"

"Oh, sure. She's really fine looking. That hair is really something. Even down here she always looks so . . . put together."

"Not as much as she'd like. At home she can't stand to be a bit dirty." I looked down at my

hands, at the dirt around my fingernails, at the scratches around my wrist, at my filthy shorts. "So, why, if she's so fine looking . . ." I rocked a little on my heels. "Why . . ." I looked up at him.

"Why did I kiss *you?*"

I nodded.

"You know, Miranda, someone can have everything all put together in the right place, be exactly everybody's idea of a ten, but there's something missing."

He paused.

"It's not the looks. It's what's behind the eyes. Something else that I don't know how to explain, but it has to be there."

Like I can't find a word for the color of this sky, I thought.

He patted the rock. "You've got it behind the eyes, Miranda." He spoke very softly and we were both quiet then for a moment.

He pulled a rock out of his pocket. "Here's something . . . for you." He held it up . . . a smooth stone that fit perfectly in the circle made by his thumb and index finger. Half of it was a deep chocolate color and the other half almost purple.

He put it on the boulder. "I know you like rocks."

"You mean I can take it?"

He nodded.

"But this is a national monument."

He held up his hand. "Don't worry. It's from the canyon behind my house. It's kind of a lucky rock, you know, that you carry around for a long time, until, you know, you decide to give it to someone else."

He looked very uncomfortable, so I picked up the rock and felt its smoothness. "It will remind me of sleeping on rocks, eating on them . . ."

"Walking with them in your shoes. Climbing them. Listen, after dinner, let's go up there. Just you and me." He pointed up at the second level of houses. "Maybe the moons are up there."

"Could Katie have gotten up there?"

"Maybe. I think there's another way up the side. I was looking at it today on our way back from the kiva. Maybe she found that way."

"Climbing a cliff in the dark. Real smart."

"We can be smart when we go back home. Come on, it's our last night to be crazy."

We both knew I'd say yes.

CHAPTER
13

DINNER WAS CRAZY. We sang and told jokes; we made toasts; we talked about Katie and the ancient people. We made plans to get together again and eat freeze-dried food. Jenny and Emily loved their sage and sweet peas and wore them in their hair. I kept my rock in my pocket and Max put the yucca blossom I gave him in the band of his hat. We were a happy group.

After cleanup, Max pointedly said that he and I were going to take a walk. Jenny and Emily cheerfully volunteered to come along. It was OK, I thought. I didn't mind us being together for a while. I knew Max and I could find a way for

the two of us to go off together. So we got ready: cameras and canteens looped around necks and strapped onto belts, boots and shoes tied up again, Max's ropes hanging from his shoulder, sweatshirts around our waists. We started off, all four of us, on what we thought was our last adventure.

Max took us down the canyon a ways, all shaded. Only the tops of the cliff still had any sun, but we had plenty of light to see our way. Not far from our camp a little draw headed around the back of the village. This was what Max thought might lead to the second level.

While he scouted ahead, we walked slowly, watching as he eased from rock to rock, looking for a way up. "That guy would worry me sick if he were mine," said Emily. "He's a super climber, but accidents happen."

"You sound like his mother," said Jenny.

I was glad neither of them looked at me. I'd been watching him, too, hoping that what he was doing only *looked* dangerous. You didn't have to be his mother to get sweaty palms when he climbed twenty feet off the ground.

"Well, that's how I feel about Max. He's just a big kid." Emily opened the journal to Katie's

map. "You know what? This place is called Ghost Draw."

"Don't tell me you're superstitious."

Emily tucked the journal pages away. "No, just careful."

I love the night, the moon, the darkness. Jenny is a sun person with her blond hair and dawn blue eyes, but I am a night person. Not only do I like to stay up late but I like to be *in* the night. More than one night during a summer I sleep out in the backyard. I love to look at the houses around me and feel superior to all my neighbors hunkered down inside.

Once I'd outgrown the chicken-and-egg story, my dad and I spent long summer nights in our backyard, he in his white lawn chair and me in my sleeping bag, finding all the summer constellations. He would tell me the stories about the bears and the sisters and the crab, and I would find other figures in the stars.

But that was backyard dark with neighbors' houses circling me and my dad's lap close if I got frightened. This night wrapped around me in a different way.

Now Max had come back down to the trail and called to us from the shadows. "There it is."

He pointed up a slope of rock. "There's a trail. If we climb up there, we'll be able to head back around and be on the second level. It's a cinch." Now I was close enough to see his grin.

"I've heard that before, haven't I?" I said.

"I don't know," said Emily. "I'm not much of a climber."

We all stared at her.

"You climbed yesterday."

"I had to. Either that or maybe drown. Only thing scares me worse than heights is water."

"Why, Cousin Emily, I had no idea you were scared of anything." Jenny laughed and put her arm around Emily's waist.

"Just don't tell anyone." Emily sat down on a rock. "Tell you what. You go up, see if you find anything, and I'll wait here. Then if it's really great, maybe I'll follow you up. Or better yet—here." She lifted the camera strap over her head and handed it to Jenny. "You take a picture if you find the moons. I don't think God Herself could get me up that slope."

"God Herself," said Max. "Give me a break." She punched him on the arm.

I looked up the slope, rock-strewn but not too steep.

"How about you, Jenny? You coming?"

"Geez, I don't know. Now that Emily mentions it, I think . . . maybe I'll just keep her company."

"Oh, go on, Jenny, if you want to," said Emily.

"No. I'm staying." Jenny handed the camera to me and then settled onto a rock beside the trail. "I'll watch you two be wonderful." Then she winked at me.

Jenny, I thought, thank you.

Max looked at me. "Well, just you and me, Miranda."

I nodded. "OK."

"Stick close to me."

Anywhere. Any time.

We both clicked on our flashlights and I followed him up the slope, watching where he stepped, how he moved across the slope. At first it was easy, a gradual rise through sage and low rocks, across patches of loose sand and packed earth. How different it was to move through the cool night, no sun to play tag with, no sweat bathing my skin. Just cool air around me.

After a time the climb got more tricky. I had to wait until Max found foot- and hand-holds, and then he waited for me, murmuring

encouragement, watching as I placed fingers and toes, correcting and praising as I worked my way up the cliff.

He reached down to me, pointing, steadying, not touching me, but I felt connected to him; a rush of energy linked us as we climbed together through the darkening air.

When it got not just tricky but difficult, enough so that I felt little flashes of fear, I wondered if this was stupid, if I might fall backward into the darkness. But of course I didn't. Max stayed even closer, gave even more exact directions, used his flashlight to show me openings in the rock I could use to move up with. At the point when I could no longer look down or up, afraid to look at anything but the rock two inches in front of my nose, when I was hearing my own panting, he said I had done it.

"Just one more step." He reached out his hand and waited until I closed mine around his. "You're here." I took a breath and lifted one foot and then the other and finally he pulled me up beside him and I didn't move away, feeling how my shoulder tucked under his, how his leg pressed the length of mine, how his hand felt warm and heavy on my other shoulder.

"You OK?"

"Yeah. That was a climb!"

"I know. More than I'd expected. Anyway, we're here."

I leaned out over the edge and shouted down to Jenny and Emily. "We're here." They waved back and shouted something.

"OK, let's go." He moved ahead, our flashlights pointed at the trail in front of us. The trail curved around the cliff and went into darkness. When we rounded a corner, I saw the sky had lightened above us as we climbed. The cliffs across the canyon began to glow.

"The moon," I whispered.

We stopped and looked back to where the canyon took a turn to the north. We watched as the moon edged up, slipped over the cliff, like a person peeking, getting braver, deciding everything was safe, then pulling herself all the way up. Below us the gulch took on light and shadow. I listened as the dark rustled and whispered.

"This is so cool," I whispered.

"Yeah," he said, "except for the snakes."

"Where?" I choked. I moved closer to him and he put his arm around me. "Do you see one?"

"Just imagine coming around a bend in the darkness with your hand out on a rock and feeling . . ." He tightened his arm around me.

"Max!"

"Don't worry." He patted my shoulder. "Snakes love sunshine—they only come out in daylight."

I pushed him away, lightly. "Don't ever do a thing like that again."

"Which thing?"

"You know."

As I followed him down the trail, I thought about how stiff and poky he'd seemed the first day with his goody-goody talk about river trips. Here he was now, being . . .

"Miranda."

He'd stopped in the trail, hand out behind him to stop me.

"No more jokes."

"No. Come on." He grabbed my hand and pulled me close behind him. I realized that I couldn't stand beside him because the trail was barely two feet wide. He stood looking up, pointing with his other arm at a spot on the cliff wall to our left.

A white face glimmered down at us from the rock.

"Ohhhh."

"Yeah," he said.

A white disk, with wide, blank eyes and a line down the middle like a nose.

"This is it," he said.

We stood and watched as the light seeped slowly off the cliff wall and the face sank deeper into the rock, the eyes showing blacker and more alive.

I thought of the person who had painted this, carrying a pot filled with water and climbing that high to paint that face. What was she thinking about as she painted? The moon she saw every month that her family used to measure time? Or the spirits that she felt all around her in this draw? The ghosts.

We didn't talk, just stood in the darkness and looked.

I touched the wall below the moon with my hand, then leaned my cheek against it. Solid and cool beneath my touch.

"I've got to get a picture," said Max finally. He pulled the ropes off his shoulder and dropped them on the trail.

I handed him the camera. "How? It's so dark."

"I think if I open the lens wide and give

it the longest exposure I can, we might get something."

"But it's too dark."

"Maybe not with the moonlight. We'll get enough to show it's here."

I brushed his hand as I passed him the camera, and he bent over it, making adjustments. I wanted to tell him to hurry, tell him to forget the photograph and think about me and us and all this moonlight.

"So you do photography, too?"

"Yeah." He grinned at me over his shoulder. "Man of many talents."

I wanted to tell him that I already knew that, but he'd turned back to the camera. He raised it once, lowered it, made another adjustment, raised it . . . lowered it. This always took so long. I stepped back so I could see the face above him, so I could see it from a few steps back, so I could tell him to come back and stand by me and we would look at the moon together. I backed up and—

I stepped into space.

One foot went and then the other and I slid over the edge, catching at the path with both hands, but nothing held me and I dropped

through air, then hit one foot hard on hard surface, then fell again, this time scraping along rock and dirt, trying to catch something, but nothing held me and I kept dropping through darkness and silence until I fell and rolled and stopped, one leg and one arm dangling into space.

I lay without moving. *I must be dead.* And I didn't want to know that yet, so I lay there, trying not to feel anything.

"Miranda!!!"

I pushed up on an elbow. The elbow held. I pushed up farther and felt agony wash me so deeply I thought I had started falling again.

"Miranda! *Miranda!!"*

"I'm . . . here."

"Where are you?"

"Here."

"I can't see you."

"I'm . . ."

"Are you hurt?"

"Yes," I whispered.

"Are you OK?"

"No!" I tried to call louder.

I bit down on my lower lip and sat up, then panted for what seemed minutes. "Oh, help," I

whispered. I straightened both legs and discovered where the pain started—in my right ankle. I reached out to it and as I straightened my arm, I felt a different kind of pain, one I remembered from falling off my bike so many times—the sting and bite of scraped skin.

"Miranda! You have to try to talk to me so I can help you."

"OK. *OK!!*"

"I'm going to drop my rope over the edge. Tell me if you can catch it."

"OK!" Shouting exhausted me and I had to lie back. The rock behind me was cool. I closed my eyes and moaned a little more, opened my eyes and saw the rope twitching in front of me in the moonlight. I reached out to it, my ankle screamed, I moaned, but I caught hold of the rope and hung on to it. Max's rope. I held it to my cheek and started to cry.

"Mira? Got it?"

I tugged on it feebly.

"OK, now I know where you are. I'm coming down."

I clung to the rope, hoping he wouldn't pull it back up. I needed that scratchy rope against my face. I closed my eyes.

Above me, I heard sounds, rocks scattering, feet slipping. Then silence. Then the same sounds from another direction.

"Don't worry, Mira. I'll get down to you. Just stay put."

I smiled just a little. Nice of him to remind me.

Then he said my name again and he sounded as if he was about to cry. "Miranda. I can't get down to you. It's too steep and there's nothing up here to tie off on. I'm afraid I'll just fall, too."

I lifted my head. "OK, that's all right. I'm all right."

"I'm sending some stuff down. Watch your head!"

A bundle dropped over the ledge and landed on my leg. My good one, thank God. Inside was a flashlight, a canteen, and the small first aid kit Max always carried on his belt.

"Miranda, you got it?"

I pulled on the rope then clicked on the flashlight and waved it in the air.

"Good! How are you?"

I ran the light over my body: arms, legs, ankle. "I hurt my ankle!"

"Can you stand on it?"

I flashed the light over my head. I had space above me to stand, so I set the light down and pushed myself upright, then slowly began to put weight on the right ankle. Pain exploded up my leg and sweat popped out all over my body. "I can't!"

"OK. You're OK. Mira, stay there, I'm going down to talk to Jenny and Emily. Don't worry, don't move, I'll be right back. All right?"

I nodded. I eased down the rock and stretched my legs out again.

"Mira?"

"Yes!" I wanted him to leave me alone. I had to concentrate on making the pain go away and I couldn't keep answering questions. I eased my legs out in front of me and lay back against the rock and panted. I opened the canteen and took a drink, then splashed some water on my face. Oohhh, cold, cold and good. I took another drink and looked out across the valley. Everything looked white and cool. I didn't want to move again, ever. I heard Max's footsteps crunch away—then silence.

CHAPTER
14

MOON AROUND ME, rocks under me, darkness below me.

I could rest here.

The night whispered in my ear and the moon seemed to warm the rock beneath my fingers.

I would be all right.

They had been here before me.

I lay in moon-shadowed space and voice-echoing time. I lay and breathed in and in, feeling for a moment as if I were drowning, as if I might never take in enough air in the white of this night.

After what seemed like a long time, I heard

Jenny's voice from far overhead. "Miranda? How are you?"

"I'm OK. I just can't walk."

I heard more voices, and I was glad I didn't have to listen to them or answer. I wanted them to leave me alone.

"I'm sending another package down. Can you catch it?"

I tugged on my signal rope, and the second rope jerked out of sight.

"Now, Miranda, don't move." Jenny again.

I nodded. "Yes," I whispered. "Yes!"

"You'll be OK. Max has a plan." I heard voices again, then Max's day pack appeared over the edge and dropped into the dirt.

"There's a sweatshirt, Mira, and another canteen. Did you catch it?"

I jerked on the rope.

I pulled on the sweatshirt. It was Max's and smelled like him. A canteen, another flashlight, an apple, a bag of gorp . . . Jenny's snacks . . . and three of Max's bandannas.

"Listen carefully, Mira. Can you hear me?"

I tugged on the rope.

"We can't get to you in the dark, so you'll have to stay there for a while. But I'll be up here if you need anything, all right?"

I tugged.

"In the morning, I'll help you get down."

I tugged.

"There's aspirin in the first aid kit. And bandages. Are you cut at all?"

"A little!"

"OK, wash the cuts with the alcohol wipe in the first aid kit. That's important."

"OK."

"Don't take your shoe off. Your foot will swell without support."

I tugged.

"I'm going to send a sleeping bag down. When you've done everything else, I want you to get in it. It's important that you don't get cold. You might be in shock. You understand?"

I tugged.

"Do everything I told you."

"Listen to Max," Jenny said.

I took two aspirin, cleaned up the worst scrapes, took another drink, pulled the sleeping bag around me, and lay back against the rock.

"OK, Mira? Need anything else?"

I shook my head.

"Mira?"

"No!"

I wanted to sink into the rock behind me; I

wanted to listen to the moon; I wanted to just be here in the night. I closed my eyes.

Something woke me.

I looked out into the dark. There, across the canyon from me, holding the light, glimmered *four* white faces, staring at me.

Shimmering in the moonlight from overhead.

Not one face—four.

Sisters to the one above me.

Four white disks, with wide, blank eyes.

Calm, cool faces.

I sat very still, arms wrapped around my body, head back against the cliff so I could see the faces across the night from me. They watched me.

"Katie," I whispered. "You *did* see these moons. You saw them, all alone. You climbed; you were brave. Were you ever afraid?"

I shook my head. I took a drink of water. I had to keep steady.

I found the end of the rope and held it to my face. Then I let it swing free.

And the girl who painted them: She must have lived a long time below this moon; she

must have come out every evening and watched the light drift across it. Then when she knew enough, she climbed all that distance to capture the moon, so sure of her footsteps, so sure of her hand on the brush that she wouldn't ever have been afraid. Someone who needed no one but herself.

I sat, still inside myself: my hands clasped around each other, one knee hard against my chest, my hurt foot cradled on Max's pack, my eyes and ears keeping watch in the night, my blood singing beneath my skin. I felt all of my body—heart, lungs, brain, skin—and I remembered Max's word: *celebrate*.

Could I say that word now and mean it? All alone and hurt on this cliffside? Could I celebrate all this? Could I be as strong as Walking Woman and celebrate pain as well as joy?

I moved my hurt foot a little and felt the throb ratchet up until I had to close my eyes and just breathe.

This place must have given a lot of pain to a lot of people. Walking Woman with her babies. And probably Katie had been burned by the sun and baked by the heat, been stung by nettles and cut by rocks.

I needed Katie and Walking Woman. What would those two brave women think of me, an almost sixteen-year-old moon- and Max-struck klutz, who'd fallen off a cliff in the dark because she wasn't paying attention?

They would understand how the moon could fill your eyes and how wanting to hold a boy's hand could be more urgent than watching where your feet were taking you. They would know and they would want to help me . . . celebrate it?

Celebrate everything. Celebrate everything so you don't forget anything. Not the heat or the pull of muscles or the thirst or the hard ground or the rain or the look of morning sun on the cliffs or the feeling of being a part of life in a way I never have been before.

The moons now smiled at me. Were they delighted that I had come?

I laughed softly at the notion, but knew once more that I was being watched.

I was here: I, Miranda Galbraith, thinking back, just as Katie must have thought back to the woman who had climbed the cliff to leave the moons. She painted the moons to speak to us when she was gone; Katie drew them in her

journal so I could find them when *she* was gone.

Ribbons of time curling forward and backward.

I opened my eyes and looked at the moon overhead.

Thank you.

Moons.

Katie.

Walking Woman and her daughter. Beloved ghost women.

Thank you.

CHAPTER
15

BY MORNING I FELT TERRIBLE. I did sleep . . .
a little, and I only know I did because I would
jerk awake, feel I was falling again, hurt my foot,
groan, and pant. When it finally began to glim-
mer light, I started thinking about the climb
down. I ached everywhere and my foot hurt
every way I moved it. My left hand was badly
scraped and my face felt pulled and sore, so I
must have scrapes there. And I needed to pee.

Then Max called to me.

"Miranda? You up?"

"Yes!"

"I'm coming down. Watch your head!"

My head? I saw what he meant a few minutes later as pebbles and then larger rocks began to scatter down the slope to my right. I ducked back under the rock. Then I saw a dangling rope and one foot and another, then his legs and then—

"Max!" I tried to reach for him, but my foot stopped me.

He got all the way down and edged into my little space and knelt beside me, half hanging into air, and put his arms around me and held on to me and said my name over and over.

Then he checked me, washed and bandaged a few scrapes I had missed. He rolled the sleeping bag out of the way, then took off my shoe. My foot was purple.

"Now you'll know why I carry so many bandannas."

He began to wrap my foot, over and around, as tight as I could stand. I held on to the side of the rocks and tried to keep quiet. When he put my shoe back on, I could feel the difference. My foot felt not normal, but not the great throbbing mass it had been, and once I edged upright and stood, I could put weight on it.

"If you're lucky, it's not broken," he said.

I wondered how bad the pain would be if it was.

"OK, now, Mira, we're going to try something. You'll have to trust me." As he talked, Max tied the sleeping bag and extra stuff into a bundle and dropped it over the cliff at the end of one of the ropes. "I've done this before, so you'll be OK."

"I trust you."

"Good."

"I don't have a choice."

"Oh, yeah, you do. You could just stay up here and hang out." All the time he talked, he was knotting and pulling at the ropes. "But then we couldn't do the other stuff."

"What other stuff?"

He pulled hard on two ropes, bracing one with his foot as I leaned against the rock and watched him. "You know, the usual, the St. George marathon and the ten-K walk and the ride-and-tie and . . ."

I groaned.

"Or maybe . . . ," he said, now tying one rope around my waist and looping the other around my legs, "just a movie and popcorn. Or a walk in the park." He pulled the ropes snug. "How about that?"

I nodded, watching his hands.

He draped a canteen around my neck and stuffed the extra bandannas in my pocket, then put everything else in the day pack and pulled it on. "We're about set. You up to being Tarzan?"

I tried not to yell like Tarzan when he lowered me over the edge, my feet dangling loose, my hands clamped like iron around the ropes that circled my chest. I dropped a few feet, then landed on a slope, but Max had warned me so I landed on my good foot. And that's the way I got down, falling a bit, landing, resting, easing off, trying to keep my bad foot out of the way— not always doing it, so I did a fair amount of gasping and grunting—but I never screamed.

After a while I heard voices again, getting closer and closer, voices calling my name.

"Go, Miranda, that's the way, do it, Mira, do it, what a girl, Mira, you can do it, Mira, almost there, wow, Mira, Mira, *Mira, Mira!!!!*"

I landed on one foot and dropped onto the dirt and sat there, grinning up at them. They fell on either side of me, laughing and hugging me and each other and then Max, once he arrived. Jenny mashed my foot once, apologized wildly, then did it again a few minutes later. I said then that I *had* to pee or I would die and that brought

us back to earth and eventually down the canyon to our camp, the one none of us had seen since yesterday.

They made a spot for me next to the stream so I could soak my foot while they went off to make breakfast. When Jenny brought me a plate, I told her I wasn't hungry.

She squatted beside me. "You sure? It may be a long wait."

"For what?"

"The rescue people. Max and Emily will hike out and—"

I hitched myself up straighter. "Who says?"

She looked surprised. "Who says what?"

"Anything about rescue people?"

"Well, it's what we're going to do. Max and Emily . . ."

I put the plate down and pushed myself to my feet. "Hey, you two," I called to Emily and Max, who immediately ran over to me, concern all over their faces.

"Listen, I'm not waiting for any rescue people. I'm going to walk out."

They both seemed to relax, as if my idea was so wild that they didn't even have to bother dealing with it.

"Hey, Mira, we have it under control," said Emily, putting her hand on my arm.

I shook it off. "No, I'm walking out. My foot is not that bad and I'm not ending this trip by being hauled out of here like . . . a sack . . . of . . . like a piece of luggage. All I need is a stick and a canteen and maybe someone to help me get my pack on." My voice started to shake a little then. I sat down.

"Miranda," Emily began, "you can't possibly walk out. You're hurt. We'll just go up, get the ranger, and be back by, oh, a few hours, and you'll be taken care of."

"I don't want to be taken care of."

"You don't have a choice."

I stood up. "Yes, I do."

I wasn't sure at all how I was going to do what I was so boldly announcing, but I was sure that I wanted very badly to do it. Jenny on one side of me, Max on the other, both of them reaching out to steady me, I stood up straighter. "I will do this and you can help me or we'll end up this trip hating each other. I have my reasons. And I know it will work out all right."

"How do you know?" said Max.

"I . . . I just know. It will be all right."

Emily looked at Jenny. "Well, she's your sister. Anything you can do?"

"Yeah. Do as she asks."

Emily lifted her hands and said, "I give up."

"OK," I said.

"How far are we from Kane Junction?" asked Max.

"A mile and a half."

"Well," said Emily, and without another word, they went off to get ready. I sank back down on the rock, my foot throbbing.

They sorted out the stuff so all I had to carry was Max's day pack and a canteen. Everyone else looked way loaded, but with no food, the packs were manageable. Max re-bound my foot and found me a good walking stick, and I took more aspirin.

"Well, let's get started," said Jenny. "Mira, it's not too late to . . ."

I ignored her. "One thing." I stopped. They all looked at me.

I hobbled the few feet to the mouth of Ghost Draw and looked down it and then up at the sides of the cliff, still dark in the morning shadows. I lifted my hand. Then I looked back at the little village, down the trail, and up the

cliffside. That last moment, she would have looked over her shoulder just before she turned the last bend up the canyon to the west. She must have looked back one last time at the little village.

I never want to do anything like that hike out again. People always talk about doing things and then laughing about them later. This was not one of those things.

This was the day: walk a ways, stop, rest, check my foot, listen to Jenny worry that it was swollen, take a drink, start again. I thought often that morning of Walking Woman and Katie, of how they were with me, just beyond my shoulder, just beyond the corner of my eye. I thought about them so I wouldn't think about the pain— the pain of my arm and shoulder when I leaned on the stick, the pain in my ankle when I hopped, the pain in my ankle when I put my weight on that foot. I lived from rest stop to rest stop, the best moment of all the one when Emily said, "Let's stop," and I could ease my bottom onto a rock and lift my foot onto a soft backpack.

When the trail started to climb, I crawled whenever I could. That didn't hurt as much. Even

so, my face was always sopped with sweat, my shirt plastered to my body, and several times I thought I might pass out.

Jenny sang and that helped, too. So did the little playlets I made up where I introduced Max to my father and mother, to my dogs, to my friends, held his hand, ran with him in the snow, danced with him, and kissed him again in the moonlight.

My foot hurt and the day was getting hotter and hotter. We stopped more and more often, and I could tell by the slant of the sun that it was afternoon. Yesterday Emily had said we would be out of the canyon by ten. Now all I wanted was to be out by dark.

Finally the slope of the trail seemed to ease. We walked a bit farther, took another rest stop, and beyond us lay the flat of the mesa.

"I'll run ahead and get the ranger," said Emily, dropping her pack. "He can bring out a truck."

"No," I said. "I've come this far. I want to make it all the way myself."

Everyone started fussing then, but I just kept walking and pretty soon they were all scrambling behind me. I felt awfully dramatic,

as if I were in a scene in a movie, but I wasn't going the last few feet in a truck.

Then it all lay behind me: the pain, yes, and the canyon we had walked through. The ranger drove the others around to the parking lot where we had left our cars. They put me in the shade, propped my foot on bags and packs, water and aspirin at the ready, a fresh apple and a bag of gorp by my side.

But I would have left it all behind me in the dust and staggered back down that narrow trail, over those white rocks edging up out of the ground like bones, back to the place where I wanted to live forever. Now I felt not just the pain from where I had fallen but the pain of longing.

I felt both pain and peace. I had followed the paths of three women I would never meet and had tried to match my mind to theirs, to see with their eyes this place they all had loved.

I found myself wanting to tell my mother all about Katie and Walking Woman. It seemed a long time since I'd had something I really wanted to tell her. This would be something. I leaned my head against the tree. Could I thank

my mother for sending me here? I didn't know. It would take me time to know.

All this was mine now, to hold on to as long as I could. I wasn't even sure I wanted to tell Emily about the moons. I knew I had to, that it was the final part of her project. Just for now, I wanted them to be mine alone.

But there, in the last moments of the journey, I made a vow: I would *not* forget; I would carry all this with me; and I would return to Katie and her beloved gulch, which now lay below the sunset, and to Walking Woman and her child, who celebrated all the beauty in their dance across stone.

For a moment I flew with the raven as she glided below the cliffs, dancing with her shadow, and then the canyon disappeared into darkness.

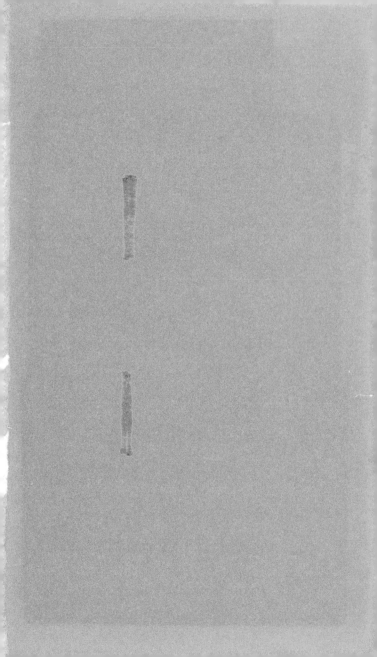

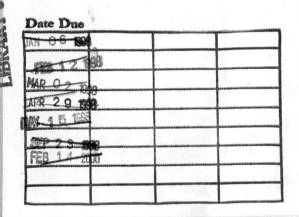